A. E. P. (Annie Eliza Pidgeon) Searing

The land of Rip Van Winkle

A tour through the romantic parts of the Catskills

A. E. P. (Annie Eliza Pidgeon) Searing

The land of Rip Van Winkle
A tour through the romantic parts of the Catskills

ISBN/EAN: 9783337046637

Printed in Europe, USA, Canada, Australia, Japan

Cover: Foto ©Andreas Hilbeck / pixelio.de

More available books at **www.hansebooks.com**

THE LAND

of

RIP VAN WINKLE

The Land of Rip Van Winkle

A TOUR
THROUGH THE ROMANTIC PARTS
OF THE
• • CATSKILLS • •
ITS LEGENDS AND TRADITIONS
BY
A. E. P. SEARING

OF

RIP VAN WINKLE

A TOUR THROUGH THE ROMANTIC PARTS OF THE CATSKILLS

ITS LEGENDS AND TRADITIONS

BY

A. E. P. SEARING

WITH ILLUSTRATIONS BY
JOSEPH LAUBER, CHARLES VOLKMAR, AND OTHERS
ENGRAVED BY E. HEINEMANN

NEW YORK & LONDON
G. P. PUTNAM'S SONS
The Knickerbocker Press
1885

Press of
G. P. Putnam's Sons
New York

" Should you ask me whence these stories,
" Whence these legends and traditions,

＊　　　＊　　　＊　　　＊　　　＊

" I should answer, I should tell you :
" ' From the forests and the prairies,

＊　　　＊　　　＊　　　＊

" ' From the mountains, moors, and fenlands,
" ' Where the heron, the shuh-shuh-gah,
" ' Feeds among the reeds and rushes.
" ' I repeat them as I heard them
" ' From the lips of Nawadaha,
" ' The musician, the sweet singer.'
" Should you ask where Nawadaha
" Found these songs, so wild and wayward,
" Found these legends and traditions,
" I should answer, I should tell you :
" ' In the birds'-nests of the forest,
" ' In the lodges of the beaver,
" ' In the hoof-prints of the bison,
" ' In the eyry of the eagle !' "　　　LONGFELLOW.

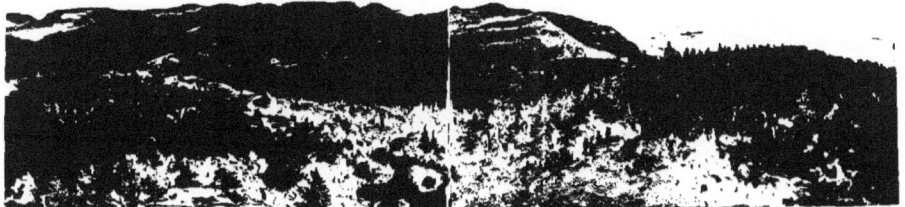

PANORAMA FROM THE OUTLOOK

CONTENTS.

LIST OF ILLUSTRATIONS

THE LAND OF RIP VAN WINKLE.

It was in September, not very long ago, that seven wise people resolved to leave the parching, blistering heat that was desolating New York—that hottest of cities—and to sail away to seek a land of cool breezes and sweet odors. Moreover, it must be some region with an atmosphere of romance to suit the Literary Fellow; it must furnish specimens for the Botanical Member of the expedition, and sketching ground for the Artist.

The Catskills, of course!

There were Mr. and Mrs. Schuyler, of Washington Square—she a pretty, well-bred woman of no particular age; he—well, he is Mrs. Schuyler's elderly husband. Then there was that pretty Miss Perkins, whose lance was always poised awaiting the uncovering of some luckless wight's weak or wicked spot, when ping! it flew straight to the vital point, and the victim was generally content to retreat and nurse his wound. As for the third lady of the party, it was enough for her that she was known as "that elegant Miss Rutherford," and her principal occupation was to go about attending to the wounded that pretty Polly Perkins left in the rear. The person most often in need of such consolation was Captain Oldbore, who had started on this trip with a goodly store of facts wherewith to instruct his fellow-travellers; practical, verified history those facts were, and he did not propose to allow the Artist

1

or the Literary Fellow to spoil them with a false glamour of romance. His theory was that history was in some sort a sacred charge, and it was every man's duty to keep fiction from usurping its place. Traditions were pernicious till authenticated, and the man most to be respected was the conscientious, truth-seeking antiquary.

Now Miss Polly Perkins cherished an ill-concealed contempt for such dry-as-dust reminiscence, and had a great weakness for the tales of by-gone days that John Grant, the Literary Fellow, had always at hand.

So one morning they all sailed away on the deck of a day-boat for Catskill. For a while the talk was all of routes and hotels until a decision was at last reached as to how much time to give to each part of the mountains. Then ensued a roll-call of baskets and umbrellas and sketching tools and other impedimenta. At last they settled themselves down to find they were approaching the Highlands, where a pulsing haze of noon-day heat covered those towering hillsides.

" How beautiful ! " murmured Miss Rutherford.

" Light's too strong," objected the Artist. " You should see them by moonlight, or later in the day, or in the early morning. They need a slanting light on them, they bear no shadows now," and with a comprehensive wave of his hand he dashed them out of the canvas, and painted them in over again.

Then the Literary Fellow took it up.

" And yet they need a haze over them ; they are never perfect without that characteristic mantle. They are loveliest in October, when Indian summer glorifies them ; then they always remind me of Captain Kidd, and those old legends."

" Yes ? " interrogated Miss Rutherford ; " I did not know the doughty old fellow's ghost prowled about here."

" Oh ! but he did come here," broke in the Artist. "Now, no doubt John there has a yarn about it."

The person thus referred to sat meditatively nursing his cane, with a far-away look in his eyes that promised a story. Miss Polly sat apart a little, where the wind was blowing her ribbons and

ON DECK OF STEAMER.

love-locks all about her face. Some of the conversation had reached her ears, for at this point she left her seat, casting a side-glance at Captain Oldbore, to make sure that he would not disturb the promised tale with cynical criticism. But there was no need for fear ; the old gentleman was deeply engaged at the moment with his historical facts, possibly " chewing a cud of erudite mistake " about

Revolutionary affairs.   All things looked encouraging as she came forward, singing softly :

> "Oh, my name was Captain Kidd, as I sail'd, as I sail'd ! "

" Do you know the rest of it ? " asks the Literary Fellow, and she finishes :

> "Oh, my name was Captain Kidd, as I sail'd, as I sail'd ;
> Oh, my name was Captain Kidd as I sail'd.
> My sinful footsteps slid ; God's law they did forbid ;
> But still wickedly I did, as I sail'd.
>
> "I 'd a Bible in my hand when I sail'd, when I sail'd ;
> I 'd a Bible in my hand when I sail'd ;
> I 'd a Bible in my hand, by my father's great command,
> And I sunk it in the sand, when I sail'd.
>
> "I spied three ships of France as I sail'd, as I sail'd ;
> I spied three ships of France as I sail'd ;
> I spied three ships of France ; to them I did advance,
> And took them all by chance, as I sail'd.
>
> "I 'd ninety bars of gold, as I sail'd, as I sail'd ;
> I 'd ninety bars of gold, as I sail'd ;
> I 'd dollars manifold, and riches uncontrolled,
> And by these I lost my soul, as I sail'd."

Mr. Grant fixed his gaze on the passing shore as if reading his legend on the green slopes, and told the story given below. Afterward it was published in the *Era*, and furnished food for many a Captain Oldbore's historical rage.   I give it as it was given to the *Era*.

THE PIRATE'S TREASURE.

In one of the old colonial mansions of New York, facing on the Battery, two men sat at a table drinking. The firelight, flaring up about the great log in the chimney, cast fitful gleams on their differing faces. The elder of the two, Colonel Fletcher, ex-Governor of the province of New York, was a man past middle life,

thin and dry, with a sharp-cut, beardless countenance, in which
were set two little bead-like eyes that seemed ever wandering in
search of evil things. Their expression belied all the suavity of the
man's face and manner; they told you that their owner was cog-
nizant of all your weakness, and perhaps of many of your pecca-
dilloes, should you conduct yourself never so discreetly, and at
some unwary moment you might find yourself in his unmerciful
clutches. His powdered peruke was arranged with the same fas-
tidious care that evinced itself in the disposition of the rich lace

CAPT. KIDD AND GOV. FLETCHER.

framing his slender, aristocratic hands. His entire person bespoke
a taste and elegance hardly removed from foppery, from his red
velvet coat, parting in front to reveal the deep lace frill on his
bosom, to the gold buckles on his shoes and at his knees. His
companion was a man of quite another stamp, and something in
his attitude as he sat with crossed knees and back half turned,
looking toward his friend only when he spoke, betokened a certain
scorn of Fletcher's foppery and ill-concealed meanness. The older

man was leaning forward with folded arms resting on the polished
mahogany of the table, keenly eying the large bulk of his guest,
as if weighing the truth of the marvellous tale he had just heard.

Of tall and finely developed figure, our hero was clothed in
some dun-colored vesture, without ornament save his decorated
sword of Moorish make, and the sash which held it at his waist.
This was of a deep-red color, and of soft silken mesh, with two
tassels at the end.   His hair was brown and unpowdered, contrary
to the prevailing fashion, and cropped closely to his head, where
it clung in little rings.   He wore long mustachios, curling up at
the ends like a Spaniard's, and his complexion was swarthy as if
browned by foreign suns, while his eyes of light gray had the absent unseeing expression that so often characterizes a person of
minute observation.   Suddenly turning to his companion, he let
his fist come down on the table, so that the glasses rung, swearing
a round oath, and concluding his malediction in some foreign
tongue.

"I tell ye, 't is a mighty treasure," he went on in tones of sup-
pressed excitement, "a Moorish merchantman bound home from
India, and richly laden, as ye may guess, with what ye already
know of such-like cargoes!"

At this insinuation Colonel Fletcher stirred uneasily, and re-
moving his eyes from the swarthy face now turned to him, gazed
into the fire.   Whether he saw there visions of gold and silver
and precious stuffs, or some new plan to help him out of his difficult situation, I do not know, but presently he stole a sly glance at
the now averted face before him.

"But, Bellomont ——," he said softly.

The eyes flashed round in sovereign contempt.   "A fig for your
Bellomont! I snap my fingers! Those six fine rubies I sent to her
ladyship, the countess, have whetted his appetite, and what though

he thundered and fumed and cast me in prison? Here I am, out
on some flimsy pardon, and those pretty baubles in his wife's jewel-
casket have changed my title from 'pirate' to 'privateer in His Majesty's service.' And yet I tell ye he 'll scarce dare to let me pass
in openly with my sloop-loads of treasure, much less let me bring
that great ship here in open sight. That troublesome make-mischief
of a Robert Livingstone too—may the Devil fly away with him!—is
growing suspicious, and must needs come posting down from his
manor to see what the Earl of Bellomont means by liberating me.
But leave that to me. I 've a trap for his fine loyal principles!
All I want of you is a well-rigged sloop and twenty sailors to go
down the coast with me where my bulky prize rides at anchor,
and help fetch away the treasure. You 'll be well paid for 't,
man!"

"Captain Kidd," said the older man, rising from his chair and
straightening his tall, spare figure, "I accept your offer and will sign
the contract. My remuneration should be heavy, for you well
know the risk I run under the new laws against harboring pirates,
should you be convicted of so grave an offence. I make this
agreement with 'His Majesty's privateersman,'" and he made an
obeisance before the bold adventurer.

"Done!" cried the sailor, starting up, and setting down his
glass so emphatically that it shivered to atoms on the table. "Have
your craft off Broecklyn, near the Wallabogt, at the first ebb-tide
on Monday next———"

"But the girl," broke in Colonel Fletcher, "I—I can't engage
to keep her on account of—of my lady."

The captain's brow darkened. "Why not, man? She 's as
honest a woman as treads the earth, and I tell ye she 's no man's
wife! I mean to marry her myself, but how can I prove the lie
on that infernal villian of a Balldridge in time to get off on my

cruise next month? He says she's a slave, and that he bought her, and I say he lies! She's a Spaniard, and as white as you are, and he stole her from a ship they took in the South Seas. I want to keep her safe from him till I come back from this one more venture."

Colonel Fletcher shrugged his shoulders and replied only : "It is a simple thing to find asylum here. As for me, my wife likes not a comely maid about the house."

" Lest she be beguiled of your fine person?" sneered Kidd ; " well, let be, I 'll not trouble you, unwilling to guard that treasure, lest I find it but ill-kept against my return."

So saying, he stalked out, with footfalls resounding on the oaken floor, and his form was soon lost in the darkness of the street. What business he next applied himself to appears in the fragment of an old document, being a letter from the Earl of Bellomont to the Board of Trade in the mother country.

" I forgot in my last letter to their Lordships to acquaint them with an arch piece of villainy done by that rogue of a chaplain whom I have since dismissed. He goes to the Lieutenant-Governor and desires him to sign a blank marriage license, pretending the parties thereto wish to keep their names concealed. The Lieutenant-Governor, suspecting mischief, refuses to do this, and my chaplain goes away. Afterward my good man brings another license, containing the names of Captain William Kidd and Isabella del Puerto, who has come, it seems, in his ship from the South Seas. Since then it transpires that he took her forcibly from Balldridge, the pirate, who says he bought her as a slave, and took her for a wife. Kidd, however, with his usual villainy, abducted her, and she is hidden past finding, for Kidd swore he would give up his life sooner than disclose her whereabouts." The letter is dated some time after Kidd's apprehension and confinement, on his return from his projected expedition just alluded to.

At noon on the following Monday a smart little craft was standing on and off shore near the Wallabogt, where soon appeared a sloop bearing down toward her. Some signals were exchanged, and the two vessels bore away to Sandy Hook and disappeared from sight of shore. Not many days after they returned heavily laden, and to the excitement and intense curiosity of the New Amsterdamers waiting on the Battery for their landing, passed on up the river, hugging the west shore, as if to baffle curious eyes. Farther up the river they cast anchor.

Just at nightfall a boat put off from one of them, and in a little while Captain Kidd was striding unobserved through the town, until he reached a place where streets converged and got themselves into a hopeless snarl. Here, turning a sharp corner, he ran bump against a man, who cried : " What, ho ! my bold captain, well met ! " and Colonel Fletcher pushed him about and gazed inquiringly into his face.

" Greeting to you—greeting ! " cried the captain impatiently. " Let me pass ! " and brushing off the detaining hand, he hurried on with a curse at this untoward meeting.

" A—ah ! " softly said the wily Fletcher, " so that is the game ! He takes his bird up river with the gold ! "

Kidd stopped at last before a low door-way, and gave a gentle rat-tat with the big brass knocker. The house was a small one, standing like most of the houses of that time with its gable-end to the street, and the entrance was through a peaked-roofed stoop, on each side of which were benches, where the good burghers were wont to sit of a summer evening and smoke the pipe of peaceful domesticity.

As our hero waited and listened for an answer to his summons, the step of a passer caused him to draw back in the shadow. While he waited, the man came opposite to him and he recognized the gait and figure of the hated Balldridge.   At the same instant a lighter step in the hallway caused his heart to leap up, for Balldridge had paused there looking up at the house.   What if the door should open and a light, held high above a lovely head, should reveal the features of her whom he was hiding from this fiend, standing here not six feet away in the darkness?   His hand reached out and grasped the door-handle, but the pirate passed on, apparently satisfied in his search.

Not long after this episode, two figures came out of the house, one muffled and veiled, the other full of anxious cares for his companion, lifting her over the puddles and rough places, pulling her shawl closer about her slender shoulders, and often supporting affectionately the lagging steps.   Once in the little boat and off for the vessel, the Spanish maiden—for it was she—seemed to revive in courage and in spirits, and all the voyage up the beautiful river she spent in gayety and happiness, with her husband, the pirate captain, or " king's privateersman," as Bellomont had now made him.

Soon he was to go on the king's bidding, by means of Bellomont, to fight the pirates in "the Red Sea or elsewhere," but on his return he would settle down in the New World with this beautiful wife, and live a new and happy life.   So they dreamed and loved each other, on this strange bridal journey, being happy and gay, for was not danger and that dreadful Balldridge behind them? and though parting was so near, it would not be very long to wait—two years at most,—and then peace and prosperity for the rest of their lives.   Meanwhile she was to find protection with an old negress whom Kidd knew, and who lived in a little house at the foot of Kaaterskill, or Palenville Clove, by the wonderful Catskills.   She could wait for him in that charming little mountain nook, and surely none could find her there.   His had

been a life of wild adventure and many daring and successful exploits, and the warm autumn days passed quickly as they sailed
along, beguiling the way with tales of the past. She, too, had
suffered privation and dangers, as stolen from her father's ship now
a year since, she had been passed over to the cruel Balldridge as
his slave, and had been rescued a few months after by Captain
Kidd, in a fight with his pirate crew in the South Sea. She had
soon learned to love her deliverer, who treated her with a gentle-
ness and deference as extreme as his harshness and severity to
others. No knight of old was ever more noble in his lady's eyes,
than this pirate of world's renown in the sight of the romantic
Spanish girl. Doubtless she made no fine-spun analysis of his
moral deviations, and to her, his seizure of other men's ships on
the high seas was no theft, but an adventure in which daring
and danger played equal parts, while crowned monarchs watched the
deeds of her hero. Now that he had promised to amend his life
and was about setting forth on an expedition as a loyal subject of
the English king, any wrong, if wrong there was in him, was
wiped away.

It is a pretty picture, of which tradition gives us but a glimpse
or hint, this brief idyl in the wild life of Kidd ; the slow sail up the
broad river in the October haze of the faded days of fall in this enchanted region. In and out of the Highlands, where Anthony's
Nose was only a high purple mountain of tremulous sunshine, and
the gorgeous foliage of many tints came down to the water's very
edge, and leaned over to see itself in the placid river ; past Esopus,
hidden up its winding creek, and so to Catskill, where, after many
calms and delays, they at last arrived, and the beautiful water-
journey was ended.

Here they lay at anchor for two days, while Captain Kidd went
among the friendly natives and settlers, trading and giving out

that he and his friends came here for the fishing and for furs which
they wanted in trade from the Indians.   On the third night there
came on board an Indian who drew the captain aside to give him
some information, and in an hour's time twenty men went down
over the side of the larger sloop into boats which were there in
waiting, and last came the Spanish girl, cloaked and veiled as before. Each man carried on his shoulders a leather sack which
seemed very heavy.

Arrived on shore they took a path leading around the village
through the woods, avoiding all observation and proceeding in
complete silence.   So they passed on over the hills toward the
mountains, coming in the early dawn to the opening of the Kaaterskill Clove.   Here the men were marched with care into a thicker
part of the forest, and their captain and the lady struck off by a
side path toward the outskirts of the little settlement.   Just where
the road coming out of the clove now divides, stood then a little
hut, where lived alone an old Madagascar negress, shunned
by the whites and the Indians.   Over the few black slaves held
then by the early settlers she exercised great power, for they
feared her and yet paid her a half-worshipful deference.   At the
time of our story, the latter part of the seventeenth century, the
old quarrels between the Patroon Van Rensselaer and the government of the colony having been long since settled, a good title
could be given to purchasers of farms in the valley, and the
holders rendered safe from the autocratic seizures of tithes and im-
posts by the old Patroon, who had tenaciously claimed the region,
and hence these rich lands were being rapidly settled and cultivated.   In the prosecution of such labors, the farmers from time
to time sent to New York, or as the Dutch still insisted on calling
it, New Amsterdam, for slaves, and in one of these consignments
had come old Dora, the negress just mentioned.   She had pre-

sented free papers, or rather a document certifying that her free-
dom had been bought, and she had given the price of her passage
to Catskill, wishing, she said, to live near the mountains. She
seemed to be supplied with money sufficient for her needs, and
wore about her unusual signs of prosperity, such as great shining
silver hoops in her ears, and a heavy string of beaten silver beads
of rude manufacture about her neck. All these peculiar circum-
stances, and her wish to live alone in a strange, far country up the
river, caused even her white neighbors to regard her with suspicion. Long years after, the story gained currency that it was
Kidd who sent her, with just the contingency in mind, that there
would come a day when she would prove useful in helping him to
conceal his treasures in these haunted hills.

To this woman Kidd took his bride, and left her with many
kisses of farewell in the tender care of the negress. The old
woman went out with him for a moment to a place behind the hut,
and there received from him certain orders and advice, and, doubtless, also good gold, and for many days after she absented herself
for several hours, saying it was at his commands. Perhaps she
was carrying the bags one by one to places of concealment on the
mountain, where some day their contents will astonish and delight
a hardy explorer, climbing up to the hidden caves and deep crevices
that seam their rocky sides. However that may be, the men must
have left their burdens to her care, for they were back on their
boats by night again without taking time to climb up through the
clove.

This treasure was the contents of one only of the sloops, and
what was done with the rest is matter of comment to this day, and
the men have been not a few who have sought them up and down
on both banks of the river. The remaining treasure was probably
buried somewhere between New York and Catskill, for the sloops

returned empty, and the rest of the goods of the Moorish merchantman were disposed of in other directions, the vessels making
no further voyages up the Hudson.

Soon after this we have records of the new compact Kidd
made with the Earl of Bellomont, governor of the provinces, and
Robert Livingston, whom Kidd had probably taken occasion to
visit on his return down the river, the Livingston Manor being
about twelve miles below Catskill, on the east bank.

Articles of agreement were drawn up between Kidd, Robert
Livingston, and Bellomont, by which the earl was to pay four
fifths of the cost of a ship to sail to " the Red Sea or elsewhere,"
and also to procure a captain's commision for Wm. Kidd, in the
royal navy, Livingston to pay the remaining fifth of the ship's cost,
while Kidd bound himself to the king's service, and if he secured
no treasure was to give up the ship on his return. The agreement begins as follows : " Whereas the said Captain Kidd is desirous to obtain a commission as captain of a private man-of-war
in order to take prizes from the king's ennemies, and otherwise to
annoy them, and whereas, also, certain persons did some time
since depart from New England, Rhode Island, New York,
and other parts in America and elsewhere, wth an intention to
pyrates and to cômit spoyles and depredations against the laws of
Nations, in the Red Sea or elsewhere, and to return with such
goods and riches as they could get, to certain places by them
agreed upon, of which said persons and places the said Captain
Kidd hath notice, and is desirous to fight w[th] & subdue the said
pyrates with whom the said Captain Kidd shall meet at sea, in
case he is empowered so to do, and whereas it is agreed between
the said parties that for the purposes aforesaid, a good and sufficient ship, to the likeing of the said Captain Kidd shall be forthwith bought, whereof the said Captain Kidd is to have the cômand."

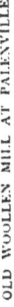

OLD WOOLLEN MILL AT PALENVILLE.

15

All of which was duly and promptly done, and in the year 1695 our gallant hero sailed away a full-fledged captain in the king's service, " with white sails flowing the seas beyond," but never more to sail the peaceful waters of the river, where awaited him his dream of love and peace and happiness. Even the dream soon proved false, and faded, for rude hands disturbed his little mountain nest, and once more sorrow hunted forth the bird it had sheltered.

In the spring following Kidd's departure, a new settler came to the valley lands under the mountains. Five hundred acres were bought near Leeds, and a large stone house, with suitable out-buildings for the cattle and slaves, erected. The owner was a stumpy, cruel-faced man, with a sun-burned, sailor look, and a manner full of vulgarity, while his speech was plentifully interlarded with oaths. He maltreated his slaves, frequently administering unmerciful punishments, such as hanging by the thumbs and tying the tongue with a tightly-drawn cord, until his neighbors shunned and loathed him. He seemed not to lack money, for he pushed the building and cultivating of his farm in a way that involved great outlay, and caused the frugal Dutch to marvel greatly, and to wonder from what land of plenty this prodigal stranger hailed. He had no family and no companion, and as autumn came on, and the work of settling was nearly finished, a loneliness and restless-ness seemed to take possession of him, and then he would wander away on his horse, spending whole days in the mountains, as if seeking some one.

Meanwhile how fares our Spanish beauty in her hiding-place ? All through the long winter she had pined and drooped, sitting sadly in the little cabin while the old negress went out on her daily ramble among the hills. Nothing could curb these restless roam-ings, not even the deep snow, for the creature had improvised a

17   VIEW FROM PROSPECT ROCK.—KAATERSKILL FALLS.

kind of snow-shoe, and on these she kept up her daily habit of wandering.   Among many other crafts she had learned shooting with the bow and arrow, and seldom returned without some small beast or bird to tempt the appetite of her guest.   Daily she tried to draw the maiden with her, but in vain ; the poor girl only shook her head sadly, and shuddered as she glanced at the snow outside.

One day the negress said to her in the fragmentary Spanish she had learned somewhere in her wanderings : " Come now, I have a great wonder to show you—only this once ; I will not ask you again."

As if to buy peace at any price, the young girl rose and suffered herself to be equipped for a mountain climb.   On snow shoes, she followed her guide up a winding trail and then over a level stretch, coming toward the amphitheatre where the fall of the Kaaterskill drops over seemingly, from one point, into bottomless space.   Clambering down the deep ravine, her mind lost in far off thoughts, the Spanish lady reached the bottom of the first ravine, when her guide seized her arm and pointed upward.   To the half-blinded eyes of this daughter of the South, who had never beheld snow and ice before this dreary winter, a miracle appeared, and, subdued by its power, she devoutly crossed herself.   From within a few feet of them rose a shining white tower of glittering ice, touching with its apex the cliff above.   Dazzled at first by the excessive brilliancy of reflection, the eyes could perceive nothing but the white blinding light of it all, but at last, accustomed to the glare, Isabel perceived through the ice walls the stream, leaping forth and breaking into spray, but perfectly noiseless.   It was a phantom waterfall, enchanted and bound in this prison of ice.   All round the circular edge of the cliff above, great icicles fell in a crystal fringe, reflecting the sunlight in all the prismatic tints, a blazing border of green and orange and rose-red jewels. Beneath the frozen lake on which the great tower stood, the stream slid silently away to the lower fall where it broke into a thousand waves, making the second cataract a great frozen wall of plunging waters.

LOOKING UP.   LOOKING DOWN.
FAWN'S LEAP.

The maiden was much moved by all this, and from that day forth, no longer declined to accompany the black woman on her rambles. As spring crept up the mountains, they fished in the swollen watercourses or hunted for sweet cresses or the flowering

arbutus. Each changing month developed some new treasure of
nature which the old woman's wood-lore readily found and ap-
propriated. So passed away the summer, and autumn found the
captain's bride more cheerful and even merry at times.

One October day the two companions were seated with their
basket beside them, on the cliff above Fawn's Leap. All the vivid
tints were on the foliage once more, and the same purple haze
through which she had sailed hither last year, was filling the heart
of Isabel with sad thoughts as she leaned back with hands clasped
behind her head. Startled suddenly by the crackling of branches
and the sound of a human voice beneath them, she sat up and
leaned forward to observe the intruder. The voice went on talking as if the man spoke only to himself : " She must be about this
clove somewhere ; Fletcher said it all went here, from that sloop,
and the girl went with the gold. A curse on the coin ! I want
the girl ! Let Fletcher find the gold for himself ! "

Isabel listened with a beating heart. The old negress had
fallen into a doze, and, seated a little way off, kept her head resting on her knees. The girl looked at her and made a rapid cal-
culation of the time necessary to waken her and escape through
the bushes ; then, looking more closely at the man below, she recognized the hated Balldridge, and all discretion fled from her, even
the power of thought, as the wild instinct of flight alone possessed
her limbs. In a moment she had sprung from rock to rock across
the stream, and was dashing through brush and brier in a blind effort to escape ; but in that moment the pirate had seen her, and,
springing up the mountain side, made short work of so unequal a
chase. He caught her near the open trail that led up through the
clove, and quickly securing her struggling form, regardless of cries
and remonstrances, to his horse which he had tied there, bore her
down to his home near Leeds, for he was the stranger who had

21   VIEW FROM THE TOLL-HOUSE AT PALENVILLE.

built the fine new house there.   Not a word did he exchange with
her till safe and fast in his stone prison he had her at his mercy,
and then the blacks told fearful tales of the sounds that issued from
the room where she was locked in.

Each day the "mas'r" would go to her, and the tones of his
voice through the closed door would sound almost gentle, as he
seemed to plead with her, but the replies were too low to be
heard.   At length his words would grow louder, and curses came
thicker and faster, while the answers were still the same ; at last,
blows and shrieks would come forth, frightening all the servants
from the house.   Presently the door would slam, and the master
would stalk forth to visit his still unsatisfied rage on whatever
crossed his path.   He said he had a runaway slave in that room,
and warned the rest not to merit a like fate.

Through all the long winter no one ever saw the face of this
runaway, but through many a night the blacks heard her footsteps
as she paced back and forth—and sometimes her sobs.   At last,
when spring had returned, one morning she was gone.   Balldridge
raged and cursed, but in vain ; no one knew aught of her method
of escape, though the blacks believed that some supernatural
power had spirited her away from her tormentor.   The tormentor,
however, had quite a different suspicion, for under the window
were two pairs of footprints, and all went in the direction of the
mountains.

The ensuing month he spent searching for the hut of the old
negress.   Somewhere in the Kaaterskill Clove he knew it must be,
though he had no certain information even of that.

Again poor Isabel was back with her old protectress, but
only a shadow of the Isabel who had been carried away the
previous autumn.   Haggard and thin, she sat all day gazing
with her great wild eyes into the fire.   Every expression, save

terror, seemed to have left her face, and that emotion was written in every line of her shrinking form. The old woman has hardly been able to leave her side since the escape, so distraught has the poor girl been at the mere idea of being alone. This morning, however, wood must be brought for the fire, and meal from a neighboring farm, so with many soothing words and charges to keep closely within doors, the negress leaves her for a few hours. Crouched down in the chimney-corner, the girl awaits hour after hour the returning footsteps. At last, soothed by the continued silence and the loneliness of the surrounding forest, she leans her poor distracted head against the bricks and dry mud that form the chimney, and falls into a deep sleep. Perhaps it is a dream of the river journey that comes to her—that voyage that seems now so far off in the past,—or perhaps it is a vision of the new life she is to enter with her gallant lover when he returns from his pursuit of the king's business. Whatever the picture may be that merciful sleep has painted, its glory has lighted up her face and fixed a smile on her lips. Some one comes creeping in at the half open door, some one steps softly over the clay floor and stands over her, and the some one holds in one hand a cow-hide whip, and in the other a coil of stout hempen cord. On the stooping face is a baleful look, more powerful, seemingly, than whip or rope, for the sleeper stirs uneasily, the light leaves her face, and she slowly opens her eyes. There is not a sound between them, and the girl presses her eyes shut with her hands as if thereby to dispel a hideous nightmare that has somehow turned up among her dream-pictures, then opens them again to behold the dreadful picture still there. Still not a sound does she make, till Balldridge raises himself and says between his set teeth :

" Get up, and come with me ! "

Then she springs away from him, throwing her arms wildly above her head.

" I will not—I will not! I will die before I go back to that dreadful house and—and you ! "

Here a shudder of inexpressible loathing seizes her and she rushes toward the door as if a remembrance of some cliff near by had suggested to her an easy method of ending the misery to come. But Balldridge is too quick for her, and soon has her bound, and is hurrying to his horse in the path below the hill. Here a brilliant device occurs to his fiendish invention, and he ties one end of the cord round her neck, attaching the other end to his saddle.

" Now, my lass," he cries, as he springs on the horse, " this time you may walk, and we 'll see if you 're in a hurry again to run away to that she-devil among the hills ! "

Whether the girl cried out, or made some backward movement, or whether indeed the spur pricked too sharply, is not known, but the spirited horse plunged suddenly, pitching his rider headlong before him, and dashed off homeward. Poor Isabel's miseries were soon at an end, for death must have quickly ensued. Certain it is that her body was dashed literally to pieces against the rocks on that awful journey, and the horse arrived at his stable with only the worn and broken cord dragging behind him.

So brutal a murder, even of a slave, found some punishment in the imperfect administration of justice in those early days. Balldridge was found guilty, but some interest, presumably his gold, softened the sentence. He was to be hung—when he arrived at the age of ninety-nine ! He was also to present himself to the judges of the court, once each year when court was in session, wearing always a cord around his neck as a memento of his crime.

So he wore out his wretched days, hated and feared by all who knew him, and in his old age they say he wore always a silken cord about his neck.

The scattered remains of the girl were collected and buried by order of the court, opposite his house-door, where a stone, telling the story of her death, should face him as he passed out. But he nailed up the door and no one ever after used it. The strangest part of his story is that he actually lived to be ninety-nine years old, though no one then could be found who would have molested the old man, already punished by a long life of loneliness and fear.

The house where he lived has been haunted ever since, and though now in ruins, it is said that in one corner where stood the room in which the hapless Isabel was imprisoned, all night long footsteps go pacing back and forth, and sobs and wails and bitter sighs afflict the night air. A great white horse with fiery eyes comes tearing down the road toward Leeds, dragging a ghastly shrieking ghost, but sometimes both horse and ghostly woman take on the form of skeletons.

As for Captain Kidd, he never returned to claim his bride. He sailed to the Red Sea as per contract, but he seems to have been unable to resist the spell of his old outlaw life, for instead of capturing the pirates, he joined with them once more. He was at last captured and taken to London, says the old chronicle, and was hanged. The last glimpse we have of him in our old New York documents is where the Earl of Bellomont falls under some slight suspicion with the Lords of Trade, of having connived somewhat at Kidd's piracies in the hope of gain for himself. Their Lordships viewed with disapproval that fine scheme of Livingstone and Bellomont to " set a thief to catch a thief," and so they set inquiries on foot, thereby worrying the Earl into shifting most of the blame on Mr. Livingstone.

In a letter to Vernon, the secretary, the Earl says : " There 's no intricacy in all that matter," and further on he continues,

" —— and ye success, I believe, had been very fortunate and serviceable, had we not been persuaded by Mr. Livingstone to put the ship under the cômand of a most aband'd villian, for we were all of us strangers to Kidd, but employed him on Mr. Livingstone's recommendation of his bravery and honesty, but he broke articles with us, for, instead of sailing direct to those seas which pyrate ships do frequent, he came hither directly to New York and loytered away several months ; and Mr. Livingstone hath told me that there was a private contract between Colonel Fletcher and Kidd, whereby Kidd obliged himself to give Fletcher 10,000 li. if he made a voyage ; Mr. Livingstone told me this was whispered about but he could not get any such light on it as to be able to prove there was such a bargain between them," —— " for mine own part I never saw him (Kidd) above thrice, and Mr. Livingstone came with him every time to my house in Dover Street."

No doubt this bargain dimly hinted at between Fletcher and Kidd was payment for the loan of Fletcher's sloop. Whatever their bargains, their sins and their frustrated dreams, they have probaby long since cleared them all up, for governor and pirate, Livingstone and Fletcher, Kidd and his Spanish maiden, had joined the great procession of " dim sheeted ghosts " many a year before we threw over our colonial governors along with that fateful tea in Boston harbor, and all other British abominations.

" Oh, thank you ! " cries Miss Polly, as the story is ended ; " I am sure I shall think of that poor girl at every spot you have mentioned in your story ! I shall not be able to climb through that ravine of the Kaaterskill Clove without a wild desire to run from Balldridge, and I shall just shi-i-ver when I see that old hut if it is still there ! "

Here a diversion was made by Captain Oldbore, who had come

up during the latter part of the recital, and who had restrained himself thus far with difficulty.

" Why, man, that 's the most absurdly inaccurate thing I ever heard ! all that about the dragging at the horse's tail is another story, and of itself was pure fabrication, you must know ! Of course as to the coming of Kidd up here, that 's likely enough, though how far up he came is not settled, but the rest, oh, pish ! "

" I have told my story," says the Literary Fellow, with a quiet smile ; " the burden of disproof lies with you."

ON THE ESOPUS NEAR PHOENICIA.

" Yes," says Miss Polly, " sit right down and begin ; no doubt we shall listen entranced ! " with which remark she walks scornfully away.

" By the way, Captain Oldbore, we must be coming to some very interesting revolutionary ground now ; no doubt this part of the river is teeming with historical associations."

The old gentleman forgets his late rebuke under Miss Rutherford's gentle influence, and forthwith launches out into such a stream of anecdote and reminiscence and statistics as rivets that lady to his side willy-nilly. On past Kingston and Rondout they sail, where the massacre of Esopus and its burning by the British are treated at length, till Catskill village approaches. The entrance to the enchanted land is not far away now, and behold, its guardian lying asleep on the mountain tops!

Nearing Catskill as you come up the river, the gigantic outlines of a recumbent Indian are traceable in the contour of the mountains against the sky. He lies on his back, with his knees slightly drawn up, and arms folded across his breast. The elongation on top of his head has the appearance of a war-plume of feathers. The attitude is imposing in its grand serenity, and on those ideal mountain days, when great fluffy clouds go chasing across their wooded sides, playing hide-and-seek with the sunshine, we can easily appreciate how distinct the personality of this giant warrior became to the superstitious mind of the savage, as the shifting lights give him the appearance of slight movement, and even cause his breast to heave convulsively betimes. Of course he had his story; what hill, or valley, or appearance in nature, had not its reason for being in the misty shadow-land of the Indian's past?

" Once on a time," Great Manitou's favorite children, the Iroquois tribes, were worrried and devoured by a giant until they could endure it no longer, neither vanquish him unaided, so they cast themselves on the mercy of the Great Spirit. They went up to his high places, and besought him, saying: "Great Father of us all, thou knowest we have done brave things! We have defended our lodges; we have given our lives; we have not been afraid; we have done according to thy command, and we are not strong enough. Oh! Chief of Warriors, slay this giant for us!"

So Manitou heard their prayer, and came among them in the form of a huge eagle, to deliver them. He found that the giant had devoured their corn so that their wives and children starved, and the breath of the dread creature was so foul that many died of wasting disease. Then Manitou engaged in a fierce conflict with the evil spirit, who had the appearance of an Indian, and at last vanquished him, but did not kill him. He, however, put him into a deep sleep, and chained him in the outline of his sacred hills, saying to his children, the tribes about their feet : "There shall he lie in slumber while ye are brave and fierce and strong, and therefore pleasing to me ; but when I am angered against my children, I will wake him again, and he shall arise and destroy all things ! "

ON CATSKILL CREEK.

Thus pestilence and famine were taken from this favored people, and chained in Manitou's hunting-ground, and heaven's sunshine, rain, and breezes brought back plenty and health to this happy region. Surely, on these wind-blown hill-tops, where, from snow till snow again, some spicy breath ever scents the air, whether of sweet-fern or flowers, or the hundred odors of the deep wood, the " Big Indian " can never wake and arise again.

Arrived at Catskill, the party was suddenly dropped into a

howling babel, whereby any sane and clear-headed person might easily have been driven to sudden insanity ; but these travellers were old stagers, used to journeyings by land and sea, and consequently not readily confused. They wended their way, uninterrupted by any alluring cries of " This way, Sir ! Cab, Sir ? " "Carriage, Sir ?—this way for Mountain View House ! " " Only stage direct to the mountains ! " With stern determination, they shook off these hackmen, who always know better than you do where you want to go, and got into the narrow-gauge train, in waiting for passengers bound for the mountains.

" There, now ! " exclaimed Miss Perkins, as they passed on, " that poor old lady who said she wanted to go to Catskill Village, has resigned herself to those demons and they will tear her limb from limb ! "

Unfortunately she had given herself to one cabby and her baggage to another, and thus chaos had ensued.

The office which the shrieking little engine resigned at Palenville, a huge mountain coach there assumed, and the party was transferred to it for the climb up the mountain side.

Oh, the loveliness of that ascent ! Out of the dust and heat, by slow toiling, surely, and yet with evident progress, into a new world of verdure and cool breezes and great silence. There was only a hint now and then of vast reaches into space, for daylight was fast fleeing, to be replaced by the glimmer of a young moon, and, as the great ark of a stage lurched around a corner where the forest was cut away, the faint touch of silver on a sea of tree-tops below made their hearts beat with a sense of the depths just beyond.

Our tired travellers slept the sleep of the weary that night, and if strange visions of Rip Van Winkle's midnight revellers visited more than one pillow, what wonder ?   Had they not seen the inn to which he returned from his long sleep in this very clove, and the old sign swinging, on their way up, and all by the witching light of the young moon?

In spite of all that they were up betimes in the morning, and assembled in the parlor by appointment to go out to an eight o'clock breakfast. But where was pretty Polly? Surely, she of all people could not be wasting this precious holiday in sleep! Indeed not, for here she comes, a great bunch of hare-bells in her hands.

RIP VAN WINKLE HOUSE.

"Aha!" she cries, "I have outdone you all, for I was up in time to see the sun rise, and see, I have a nosegay with mountain-dew on it.

Breakfast over, the next thing to do is North Mountain with its views. The day was one peculiarly characteristic of the mountains, hot, but with an occasional cool breeze to pat the cheek with a slightly frosty touch, and little white clouds sailing over the bluest of skies.

Toiling up the steep slope near Captain Oldbore was a stout old German gentleman with a pleasant, beaming face, out of which a pair of mild blue eyes looked through very short-sighted glasses. At some exclamation of surprise, he took occasion to say, " Then it ees thet you are strange to these mountains ? "

Being assured that such was the case, he continued :

" Oh, it ees not so with me! I am goming here now these dwenty years, and it is dangerous eff you will pe glimbing. It is many soomers I hev carried pendages und leeniment in my

THE OLD GERMAN.

pockets for an eccident "—here he displayed a neat roll of linen and the bottle.

" What a dreadful apprehension ! " shuddered one of the ladies.

Back toward the west, the view from the North Mountain is very fine, and no feature in it is more lovely than the tiny lakes nestling down in the shadows. On the dullest days they catch some remnant of light and flash it back to the hill-tops. Mrs, Schuyler felt that she could not go home without a nearer exploration of those lakes.

" Better not ; you won't find them so pretty nearer by, probably nothing but boggy little mud-holes."

VIEW FROM NORTH MOUNTAIN.

33

It was the Artist who spoke, and his temerity was promptly punished by the general expression of a determination to investigate those bodies of water while at the Kaaterskill Hotel.

In the afternoon they transferred themselves to that house. There the ladies seated themselves on the broad veranda, while the male members of the party were absent in conclave with that august person, the hotel clerk.

The rueful groups soon returned, headed by Mr. Schuyler.

THE DUDE.

" Well, my dear," said that over-heated and rubicund individual, "I guess we 're in for it. They 're all here—the Carrolls, the Beekmans, and fifty more—besides, there 's a hop to-night."

This last was added tentatively, in some fear of that imperious little lady who ruled his skies, for well he knew her aversion to summer parties and other full-dress frivolities in the " heated term." Each summer she carried off her submissive spouse to a pleasuring like this, with a few chosen spirits, for a rest, after the long winter when she served her turn at Society's wheel with the other

ON THE ROAD FROM KAATERSKILL HOTEL.

social slaves.   Now she leaned back in her chair and fanned
herself gloomily.

Alas! the futility of those pretty dresses in the trunks!   Each
lady had brought a gown suitable to meet just such a possible contingency as this, but it was carried much as one takes an um-
brella on a cloudy day, with a defiantly-held superstition that it
may scare off the rain.   Miss Rutherford, too, looked bored, but
Miss Polly cried gayly, " Why, that 's delightful ! "

So the hop came off, bringing pleasure to one of the ladies at
least, and our pilgrims made their entrée once more into New
York and Philadelphia and Boston at once, in the great drawing-
room which seemed large enough to hold the entire population of
the last-named city.   All the many friends came flocking about,
and the mutual surprises and greetings and exclamations were very
numerous.

There was a band, of course, and waltzing, and some flirtation,
no doubt, while just outside the long windows the moonlight had
flooded the great world beneath their feet.   Surely in that enchanted land down there, all wrapped in a silver mist where a
shining ribbon wound along through the dim light showing the
course of the river, surely there was no care, nor sorrow, nor heart-
ache.   What a wonderfully beautiful world it is after all, and how
the cynics have abused it !   A faint odor steals up through the still
air, the moonlight has a kind of throb in it ; verily those hills, rising
far away there in the east, must be the Delectable Mountains.   Here
an " ill-boding crow," awakened from his midnight slumbers, comes
flapping and croaking up the gorge, a window opens on the quiet
corner and two people step out, bringing a flare of gaslight, the
sound of brass instruments, and a scrap of society comment.

" You think her so quiet and pretty?   I assure you her conduct has been the gossip of the house this month past ! "

VIEW FROM SUNSET ROCK.

37

Wake up, old world! You are an arrant humbug, no Arcadia after all, but just the same old evil-thinking and evil-speaking world you were before.

In the morning there was an energetic scramble over rocks and hills and through rocky ravines. Who can tell what those seven people saw from Sunset Rock ? Each through his own mood saw his own picture, and long he never so deeply, not one peep could

ALIGATOR ROCK.

he get of what his neighbor might be finding there at the same moment. In the shifting lights and shades, the deep greens and suggestions of coming autumn, the Artist found much for his work, and carried home with him more than his portfolio held, while I doubt if Miss Rutherford's herbarium contains half the blossoms she picked by the way ; as for the Literary Fellow, much was brewing in his head, of which he afterward gave to others but a portion, and

THE LAKES.

that perhaps not of his best, for what is best in artistic impressions seldom gets translated after all, so that a man's work is always just behind his effort.

As for the tiny lakes they proved to be as lovely as they had promised. Nestling down between the surrounding peaks, they seemed fit abodes of peace. Around their shores tall reeds, cat-tails, calamus, and many others are ever nodding and bowing before

SHELTERING ROCK.

the little breezes that shiver over the bosom of the water, while tall trees lean over as far as they dare in the marshy foothold, and throw deep shadows where trout can hide safely and water-fowl float secure in the early spring.

Here these people rested in the shade, while the energetic Miss Polly and John Grant went cleaving the water in a sharp-nosed little boat after water-lilies that floated far out in mid-channel.

Already there were forewarnings of a shower, at which they all rejoiced greatly, for a storm on these mountains gave promise of great beauty and grandeur entirely new to them. The necessary thing to do, therefore, was to make all haste to begin the prospective drive down to Palenville, for they were going there
to engage rooms for the following day, and they wanted to observe the progress of the storm
from the new road that leads
down the mountains from the
Kaaterskill House.

Midway on the descent the
storm burst upon them, so the
covered wagon drew up at one
side of the road beneath some
overhanging trees, and the inmates arranged themselves to
enjoy the shower and yet preserve dry clothes. With a tre-
mendous crashing and booming
it came tearing down the narrow
gorge. The rain seemed to ad-
vance in a gray column reaching from the earth up into

IN CAUTERSKILL CLOVE AFTER RAIN.

the darkened heavens, and the wind rushed along as if through a funnel, with a fury redoubled from being confined by the mountain sides. The trees bent low their bared heads, their branches and leaves flying before the blast. The noise of the thunder was deafening as it reëchoed from side to side of the deep ravine. As the storm was fierce, so it was of short duration, and soon the rain-cloud seemed to have passed over, while the sun broke forth above the waiting travellers, shining on the shower that was now beneath their feet. As they passed on down to the valley the trees, the wayside weeds and dripping vines, the very stones, glistened and

ARTIST ROCK AND PALENVILLE OVERLOOK.

shone under the dancing sunlight, while below them the clouds were scattering in little puffs like smoke, and distant mutterings brought word that the spectacle was over.

Down they go rattling over the stones at a great pace, for Palenville and dinner are ahead and much must be done yet this day. Quarters secured for the night, arrangements made about receiving the baggage that is to be sent down, and dinner eaten with great zest but short ceremony, the horses are put to the wagon and they again ascend the mountain, this time by the old Kaaterskill Clove road, with the design of walking back through the ravine. " To the Laurel House," the order is given, and there is the chief delight of the day, for there is the sanctum, or rather the prison and keep of the far-famed " Kaaterskill fall."

" How prosaic—how vulgar!" cries Mrs. Schuyler, "to walk down wooden steps in a spot like this! Oh, I really can't—I much prefer clambering down some other way!"

MARY'S GLEN NEAR LAUREL HOUSE.

43

" Well, you 'll think differently when you come up," suggested her husband.

Down at the bottom of the ravine they look up at the amphitheatre almost covered with dripping mosses, and fringed at top with drooping pines. It is all very lovely, but pretty Miss Polly voices a general sentiment when she exclaims disappointedly :

" Is that all there is of it ?   That little thread of water ? "

Indeed it did seem a very little stream to make such a fuss about. The Artist smiled ; he had been here before and knew the trick.

" Come down," he said, " under the lower fall, and then look up."

From that point the little house built just above the precipice looked like a tiny bird-cage.

" Oh, look now ! " cries Miss Polly clapping her hands with pleasure.   High up in the air a white cloudy mass springs far out and falls in a foaming torrent.   Down, down it comes till at the foot of the first fall it strikes the glassy surface of the pool, and rushes through it like a white snake.   Over the second and smaller fall it comes and falls at their very feet in a drenching shower of spray.   It is a humiliating thought that this beautiful mountain stream should be dammed up and turned on at twenty-five cents a piece for the lovers of nature, but we should have only the little thread of water all summer otherwise, whereas now for a consideration we get all the majesty of the spring floods let on.

" It must have looked like that the first time it came down over that rock."

" What do you mean ? " said Miss Rutherford, looking for his explanation to the Literary Fellow ; " was it not always here ? "

" You do not then know the legend ? "

" Tell it—tell it ! " demands Miss Perkins eagerly, while Captain Oldbore looks impatient at such an absurd proposal.

" It is too long to tell now, but this evening, if you wish – "

45   ON TOP OF HAINES' FALLS.

"Of course," breaks in Mrs. Schuyler, "the shower has cooled the air so that we shall need a fire on the hearth this evening, and I saw a place for one at our boarding-house. That will be just the thing!"

DRIPPING ROCK.

Captain Oldbore said something about a little paper on revolutionary days he had hoped to read them to-night.

"By all means," consents the amiable lady, "we will make that sort of thing the feature of our evenings."

Miss Perkins is no longer able to restrain her feelings at the prospect of an evening with what promises to be a dreary feast of facts.

"Now, my dear captain, this region is sacred to the Indian, and I must beg that you will not intrude your pushing and uninteresting whites till we are safely at home!"

Miss Rutherford averted any further trouble and smoothed down the old man's ruffled vanity by calling him aside to give an opinion on the family name of a pretty vetch that clung to the rocks near by.

Now for Haines' Falls and that gorge, stopping by the way at Dripping Rock and at the Land Slide for the prettiest of views

47   HAINES' FALLS

down the winding clove. At Hainesville the wagon is dismissed
and they begin their scramble down through the rocky gorge.
Fawn's Leap, Buttermilk Falls, and Belle Falls come each in turn,
and each holds its own peculiar attraction undimmed by the rest.
Not far from Palenville the ravine widens into a little valley, and
the stream is bordered by wide stretches of green turf. Square
ridges of green grass surround old cellars partially filled with rub-
bish, over which wild blackberry vines run riot and cover the un-

ARTIST GROTTO.

sightliness. Golden-rod and purple asters choke the doorways,
and clumps of old-fashioned garden annuals mingle their sweet-
ness with the tall grass ; sweet-williams, pinks, and now and then
a shrub, where the path must have led to the door. This is a
veritable " Deserted Village," and here Captain Oldbore's facts
began to prove useful. He told them it was the ruins of an old
tannery with its settlement of workmen's cottages. Tanning

THE CASCADES OF HAINES' FALLS.

hides was once the most flourishing industry of all this region, but as the hemlock bark was exhausted it died a natural death. Acres upon acres of trees are felled, stripped, and left, the parching summer wind dries the dead wood to tinder, and then some chance spark sets going a conflagration that sometimes lasts for weeks in the autumn gales.

"Sir," concludes the excited captain, now in full tilt on one of his hobbies—"Sir, we are a most unthrifty, wasteful people! Thus, from year to year, we recklessly devastate our forests, lay bare the sources of our streams, and so are gradually changing the climate itself!"

Pleasant, indeed, was the fire that night as they all gathered about it in the big Palenville boarding-house. There was a frosty touch in the air and they spread their hands to the blaze with a genuine sense of comfort.

"Now for the legend, Mr. Grant," and Mrs. Schuyler settles back in her comfortable chair; "you know you promised!"

And thus, by the flickering light of a fire on the hearth, they listened to

THE BIRTH OF THE KAATERSKILL.

"A legend that grew in the forest's hush
Slowly as tear-drops gather and gush,—

*   *   *   *   *

It grew and grew,
From the pine-trees gathering a sombre hue,
Till it seems a mere murmur out of the vast
Norwegian forests of the past."—LOWELL.

In the far off days behind us, in the time when legend and fairy tale and childhood's lore was true, when every cave, and ravine, and waterfall had its spirit, good or evil, these mountains were sacred ground to the superstitious Indian, and it was with wary steps and fearful heart he explored their secret places for

LAND SLIDE ON TOP OF CAUTERSKILL CLOVE.

51

wild beasts, and the shyest birds of the wilderness. Here the great
Manitou held sway in a high place, and sent forth his emissaries
in the lightning and thunder, or the balmy west winds that draw
down through their cloves sometimes on a sultry midsummer day.
Held in the highest veneration, no human quarrels were allowed
to intrude on Manitou's battle-ground, and however loud he might
thunder and war on stormy nights, as his approving spirits clashed
in warfare, on this sacred ground the red man's scalping-knife was
sheathed, and his arrow never found here its way to any human
heart. Seldom, indeed, did the Indian come up here, save to hunt
the bear or catamount, or to cross over through the Palenville
clove trail to make war on the peaceful Catskill natives.

Along the river the Indians were more peaceful than the war-
like tribes of the six nations, who dwelt beyond the mountains,
spread over all the country to Lake Erie on the west and Ontario
on the north. The peaceful river-dwellers cultivated plantations
of corn and beans, and lived, according to the accounts of early
navigators who explored the Hudson, a quiet and somewhat
domestic life. They were of the great Mohican nation, and held
a tradition of an origin in the west where their enemies, the Mohawks, now held sway. This tradition preserved among them,
caused them to resent with intense bitterness the marauding wars
of the tribes from beyond the mountains, who made occasional de-
scents upon their fertile fields, destroying sometimes a year's work
in a day, and murdering or killing all they could catch, while the
children they carried away in captivity, to be brought up as
Mohawks themselves.

Hendrick Hudson, in his account of his voyage in the "Half
Moon" in 1609, gives some descriptions of these people and of
their habits.

He says: "At night we came to other high mountains which

BELLE FALLS AT PALENVILLE.

53

lie from the river-side. There we found very loving people, and very old men where we were well used. Our boat went to fish, and caught great store of very good fish.

"The sixteenth, fair and very hot weather. In the morning our boat went again to fishing, but caught very few, by reason their canoes had been there all night. This morning the people came aboard and brought us ears of Indian corn and pompions (squashes) and tobacco ; which we bought for trifles. We rode still all day and filled fresh water ; at night we weighed and went two leagues higher, and had shoald water ; so we anchored till day."

At Schodac, he enters in his journal the following : " I sailed to the shore in one of their canoes, with an old man who was chief of a tribe consisting of forty men and seventeen women. These I saw there in a house well-constructed of oak bark, and circular in shape, so that it had the appearance of being built with an arched roof. It contained a great quantity of maize, or Indian corn, and beans of last year's growth ; and there lay near the house, for the purpose of drying, enough to load three ships, besides what was growing in the fields. On our coming into the house, two mats were spread out to sit upon and some food was immediately served in well made wooden bowls. Two men were also dispatched at once, with bows and arrows, in quest of game, who soon brought in a pair of pigeons which they had shot. They likewise killed a fat dog, and skinned it in great haste, with shells which they had got out of the water. They supposed I would remain with them for the night ; but I returned in a short time on board the ship. The land is the finest for cultivation that I ever in my life set foot upon, and it also abounds in trees of every description. These natives are a very good people, for when they saw that I would not remain, they supposed that I was afraid of their bows ; and taking their arrows, they broke them in pieces and threw them into the fire."

So it was these "very loving people" of the river, above Esopus, the Catskill Indians, lived in peace and prosperity under their chief Mayna, cultivating their lands and handing down to their children the traditions of their forefathers, in which lore their tribe, the Mohicans, were rich.

Not so, however, with their enemies, the Mohawks, beyond the mountains. With them the art of war was imbibed with the mother's milk, and all their tales about the fires were of blood and battles, and the adventures of the braves with their enemies. Their education was devoted to the development of endurance and bravery, and their religion, like most of the Indians, was chiefly a placating of the dread Manitou and the various demons and giants that waged unseen war against them. High Peak was the home of the Great Spirit, and the woods around it a sacred grove where once yearly they came to perform their religious dance about a huge fire at midnight. Tradition says that in the far-away past, when there was no water in Palenville clove, that part of the mountains was the favorite hunting-ground of Manitou ; and indeed, after a climb through that fairy-like region on a bright June day, the super- stition is easily believed. Nature seems to have made a peculiar effort to adorn each rock and tree and wandering pathway with lichen and moss and vine and delicate maiden-hair fern. All shades of green are these, ever shifting and changing as the leaves stir and glisten, with inter-lines of fine gray moss, and the blood-red splashes of liver-wort on the varied carpet under foot, while all about are hiding branches of blossom, white and pink or vivid scarlet ; it is a fugue in colors—a soul-stirring harmony, that repeats itself in echoing refrains all writ in nature's pigments. Here, great Mani- tou walked at noon-day undisturbed, for in that remote time, no trail was made through this clove.

Now among the western tribes beyond the mountain appeared a great wonder—a snow-white maiden with flaxen hair and blue eyes! Their chief, when away alone, on an expedition to prove his prowess, had found her, he said, beneath a tree, down in the South-river (Delaware-river) country, wrapped in white blankets of exquisite fineness. The little one was looked upon as a gift from the Great Spirit, an omen of his favor, and was forthwith treated as a goddess. No goddess could wed with mortal man, so she was vowed to virginity, and once a year was taken to Manitou's mountains, and in the sacred clove left for a week to his holy protection and ministration. This ceremony, however, was not inaugurated till her eighteenth year.

As she was clothed in white when first found, they continued to make her garments of that hue, and "The White Maiden " was her title. Very beautiful she was said to have been, and wise as well, for her advice was asked as if she were an oracle, and her commands were followed with fidelity.

One May-time they carried the maid to the sacred spot, placing in her lodge made all of white skins, procured at great pains, cakes of maize, meat, and lentils, and then they went away and left her weeping at her lonely plight. Not long did her tears flow, however, for soon a slight noise in the forest startled her, and springing up in terror she espied, approaching, a beautiful youth of some tribe unknown to her. Making signs which all Indians, even of widely separated tribes, readily comprehend, he assured her of his good-will, and promised to protect her in her lonely stay. Her fears at rest, she listened to him, and soon learned to love him, and hand in hand they wandered through the beautiful region like happy children. So they remained in the joy and inno-cence of childish love till the time drew near for the warriors of the Mohawks to reclaim her ; then the strange youth departed,

promising to come to her at this time the following year, and en-
joining on her strict secrecy. They made their farewells with many
tears, and the beautiful stranger disappeared down the clove, going
toward the river. On the morrow the Mohawks took away the
White Maiden, and from the new look of happiness in her tear-
stained eyes they guessed she had seen the great Manitou, her
father, and forebore from questioning her. For several years this

DELAWARE VALLEY.

idyl was repeated, till at last the youth one May-time found himself unable to tear himself from the side of his mountain love, and
so disaster came upon them.

Lingering with her till the last day, he persuaded her to go
eastward with him to his own people and there to abide, and she at
last consented. Wandering thus away from the white lodge they
forgot in their love and happiness the danger of detection before

leaving the mountain, and the Mohawks, finding the lodge deserted, separated to search the mountain side for their lost goddess. One of these searchers spied the lovers sitting on a mossy bank, and immediately ran to tell his companions. Just at this time the beauty was imposing a task on her swarthy lover ; it was to bring her, from a point far down the rugged ravine, a bunch of blue-bells she had noticed there a short time before, hanging over a dizzy height. The youth sprang down from stone to stone, clinging here and there to overhanging branches and was soon lost to sight. Stillness reigned in the shaded chasm, and the leaves cast little flecks of moving shadow over the white leggings and snowy blanket of the girl, and her long wavy hair fell in a golden shower down her back. She leaned forward, watching the dense growth below for some sign of moving branch, and listening for a sound of cracking twig to give token of the youth's return. Suddenly a wild yell above her re-echoed from side to side of the rock-bound ravine, and seemed enclosing her in a mad babel of sound. Starting up, she stood a moment with her hand pressed to her breast, then seeing the advancing Mohawks as they came rushing down the mountain, she seemed to divine with quick instinct what they were seeking, and the hideous punishments that awaited her lover, if he were caught. Instantly she turned and darted down the clove like a flash of white light as the sun shone on her garments where the shade divided as she passed. Down, down, and the quick feet behind her coming nearer, while the savage cries seemed in her very ears ! Much farther she cannot go, for here is the precipice of the Kaaterskill, descending straight across the vale with sheer fall into dark, stony depths. Springing to the rocky platform, at its edge she paused and turned, her blanket partly falling from her gleaming shoulders, then, as if with sudden resolve, as the yells came nearer, and the hands of her friends were stretched out to save her, she sprang into mid-air, her hair streaming out behind her and mingling with the folds of her blanket. And now a great marvel came to pass, for before their eyes, dazzled by the sun-illumined garments, the maiden disappeared in a stream of water that plunged for the first time in the memory of man, over the cliff, and went rushing down the gorge in white tumbling foam. It seemed to them that the snowy garments faded and melted into a myriad glistening drops of spray, and the floating yellow hair became the golden bars of sunlight on the water. So the great spirit took his daughter to himself, and the saddened and awe-struck savages went their homeward way, not daring now to wreak their vengeance on the Catskill chief who caused all the trouble. But they never

THE MAID IN KAATERSKILL FALLS.

forgot, says tradition, the old score against the river Indians, and, till civilization drove them westward, they continued to wreak their vengeance on their enemies.

It is all a myth, of course, and yet at times by the witching light of a midsummer moon, if you tune your thoughts aright, the silvery white garments seem to gleam through the waters of Kaaterskill, and the face will almost shape itself, then fade away ; while the dripping, floating hair is often present near the top, before the water breaks in a misty veil of spray.

There existed among the Indians when the first whites came to them a tradition that in early times a vessel had been wrecked on the Atlantic coast and most of the crew drowned. The few who survived were pale of face, with flaxen or golden hair, and soon mixed with the tribe of the Tuscaroras, then inhabiting Virginia. The Tuscaroras afterward moved northward and came to western New York, still preserving this tradition of pale-faces. The two stories would seem to have some dim connection, and it is not beyond credence that Manitou's " White Maiden " was the deserted baby of some Northman of old.

Amid the various comments on this tale, Captain Oldbore surprised every one by a gracious corroboration of part of it, which was the more to be wondered at because he had listened to its recital with evident impatience.

" Now, that interesting fact about the ice-formation under the fall is strictly true, and may be observed toward the latter part of February or early in March, when the slow accretions of frozen drops of spray have built a circular wall around the place where the water drops into the pool, but the instances of its reaching the top of the cliff are rare, though I have spoken with more than one mountaineer who has seen it."

Mrs. Schuyler said civilly that " she hoped the story would soon appear in print," and Miss Rutherford was reminded of Bryant's verses on the Kaaterskill, which she recited :

Midst greens and shades the Caaterskill leaps
    From cliffs where the wood-flower clings ;
All summer he moistens his verdant steps
    With the sweet light spray of the mountain springs,
And he shakes the woods on the mountain side,
When they drip.with the rains of autumn-tide.

But when, in the forest bare and old,
    The blast of December calls,
He builds in the starlight, clear and cold,
    A palace of ice where his torrent falls,
With turret, and arch, and fretwork fair,
And pillars blue as the summer air.

For whom are those glorious chambers wrought,
    In the cold and cloudless night ?
Is there neither spirit nor motion of thought,
    In forms so lovely and hues so bright ?
Hear what the gray-haired woodmen tell
Of this wild stream and its rocky dell.

'T was hither a youth of dreamy mood,
    A hundred winters ago,
Had wandered over the mighty wood,
    When the panther's track was fresh on the snow.
And keen were the winds that came to stir
The long dark boughs of the hemlock-fir.

Too gentle of mien he seemed, and fair,
    For a child of those rugged steeps ;
His home lay down in the valley where
    The kingly Hudson rolls to the deeps ;
But he wore the hunter's frock that day,
And a slender gun on his shoulder lay.

And here he paused, and against the trunk
    Of a tall gray linden leant,
Where the broad clear orb of the sun had sunk
    From his path in the frosty firmament,
And over the round dark edge of the hill
A cold green light was quivering still.

And the crescent moon, high over the green,
    From a sky of crimson shone,
On that icy palace whose towers were seen,
    To sparkle as if with stars of their own,
While the water fell with a hollow sound,
'Twixt the glistening pillars ranged around.

Is that a being of life that moves
    Where the crystal battlements rise?
A maiden watching the moon she loves,
    At the twilight hour, with pensive eyes?
Was that a garment which seemed to gleam,
Betwixt the eye and the falling stream?

'T is only the torrent tumbling o'er,
    In the midst of those glassy walls ;
Gushing, and plunging, and beating the floor
    Of the rocky basin in which it falls.
'T is only the torrent—but why that start ?
Why gazes the youth with a throbbing heart ?

He thinks no more of his home afar,
    Where his sire and sister wait ;
He heeds no longer how star after star
    Looks forth on the night as the hour grows late ;
He heeds not the snow-wreaths,—lifted and cast
From a thousand boughs by the rising blast.

His thoughts are alone of those who dwell
    In the halls of frost and snow,
Who pass where the crystal domes upswell
    From the alabaster floors below,
Where the frost-trees bourgeon with leaf and spray,
And frost-gems scatter a silvery day.

' And oh ! that those glorious haunts were mine ! '
    He speaks, and throughout the glen

Thin shadows swim in the faint moonshine,
  And take a ghastly likeness of men,
As if the slain by the wintry storms
Came forth to the air in their earthly forms.

There pass the chasers of seal and whale,
  With their weapons quaint and grim,
And bands of warriors in glittering mail,
  And herdsmen and hunters, huge of limb ;
There are naked arms with bow and spear,
And furry gauntlets the carbine rear.

There are mothers, and oh ! how sadly their eyes
  On their children's white brows rest !
There are youthful lovers—the maiden lies
  In a seeming sleep, on the chosen breast ;
There are fair, wan women, with moonstruck air,
And snow-stars flecking their long loose hair.

They eye him not as they pass along,
  But his hair stands up with dread,
When he feels that he moves with that phantom throng,
  Till those icy turrets are over his head,
And the torrent's roar as they enter seems
Like a drowsy murmur heard in dreams.

The glittering threshold is scarcely passed,
  When there gathers and wraps him round
A thick white twilight, sullen and vast,
  In which there is neither form nor sound ;
The phantoms, the glory, vanish all,
With the dying voice of the waterfall.

Slow passes the darkness of that trance,
  And the youth now faintly sees
Huge shadows, and gushes of light that dance
  On a rugged ceiling of unhewn trees,
And walls where the skins of beasts are hung,
And rifles glitter, on antlers strung.

On a couch of shaggy skins he lies ;
  As he strives to raise his head,
Hard-featured woodmen with kindly eyes
  Come round him and smooth his furry bed,

And bid him rest, for the evening star
Is scarcely set, and the day is far.

They had found at eve the dreaming one
  By the base of that icy sleep ;
When over his stiffening limbs begun
  The deadly slumber of frost to creep,
And they cherished the pale and breathless form,
Till the stagnant blood ran free and warm.

Next morning the skies are gray, and a cold, soaking rain is
falling. The disappointed pleasure-seekers look forth from behind their windows and conclude to give up all open-air plans and
stay within doors warm, at least, and dry. The fire is alluring,
and one by one they settle down for a morning with books and
work and talk. Mrs. Schuyler is busy over a bit of knitting that
she calls her " kill-time," but which her husband has dubbed " the
spoil-sport," as he dreads with true masculine hostility her absorp-
tion in its mysteries. Miss Rutherford is arranging her botanical
specimens, while pretty Miss Polly is pulling the ears of a gray
pussy-cat in her lap, and rubbing it gently under the chin. The
Literary Fellow is occupied with watching this performance, while
the Artist is making sly sketches of each one from his corner. As
for the captain—not long since a dangerous gleam shone in his
eye as he rose and stole quietly from the room. Now he returns
with a neat roll of manuscript in his hand, at the sight of which an
uneasy stir runs through the party, and Miss Perkins groans
audibly.

" I thought it an excellent opportunity to read you my pages
on the ' Revolutionary Captivities.' In a few days more we shall
be going through the river valley again, and that region as well as
these mountains is concerned in the stories."

Of course he was politely urged to read, so unrolling his papers, he began at once.

REVOLUTIONARY CAPTIVITIES.

It was the custom of our English cousins, in the early days of revolt and trouble with the colonies, to use with unstinted zeal the hate and cruelty of the red man as weapons against their rebellious subjects. If the atmosphere be permeated with a subtle magnetic fluid, as some spiritualists assert, on which passing events are photographed in gesture and grouping of figures, then, to him who has the "second sight," the valleys of the Hudson and Mohawk

GEORGE HALL'S HOUSE.

rivers unroll one long panorama of human agony. Rapine, arson, and murder marshal their forces in the ghostly procession. Wild arms are raised to heaven in vain appeals for help. Women and children are fleeing from demons in war-paint and feathers who are in hot pursuit, while the smoke from burning barns and homesteads seems to rise like incense to the heathen gods of War and Death. Give voice to this phantasmagoria of horrors, and what a wail of agony goes up in accusation! Who was to blame?

Perhaps the captivities were a degree worse than immediate murder, for in the one case there ensued the long march through the great forests and across mountains and rivers to Canada, where,

if the wretched one lived to reach that destination, there awaited
him impressment into the British service, or an imprisonment
whose horrors were equal to his previous tortures by the savages;
in the other case the tomahawk was at least a merciful shortening
of the death.

About two miles west of Catskill lived in those troubled days
the Dutch family of Schermerhorns. One son had married a
daughter of Mr. Scrope, who lived on Roundtop Mountain. Another son, Frederic, was one day sent to the mountain where
his brother had taken up his abode with his wife's people to obtain
his services in helping to get the Schermerhorn sheep driven
down from their mountain pasture. Arrived at his destination,
and greatly wearied from his long day's journey, he soon retired
to rest. In the early morning he was aroused by the screams of
his sister-in-law, who was alarmed by the appearance of some
Indians who were approaching the house. Long afterward, in
telling the story to his children Frederic used to recall how his dog
had howled when he left home the day before, and then he would
add : " Mine kindern, petter stay to home ven te dog howls!"

Drawing on his clothes quickly he ran down stairs to find the
family in great alarm. Mr. Scrope had been at work in the fields
but was coming back to the house now, having seen the approach
of the savages. Meanwhile the warriors seemed friendly enough
with their " How-do's" and inquiries for Bastyon, a son of the
house who was then absent in Saugerties. It was afterward
thought that their object in coming was to seize and kill this
Bastyon, who had once served them a mean trick in stealing from
them some hatchets and knives. Finding their inquiries for
the delinquent to be in vain, they concluded to satisfy their grudge
in some other way, and so began plundering the house, thereby
trying the frugal soul of Vrouw Scrope, who wept and fumed to no

good purpose. One brave, possessed of unusual discernment spied the linen-chest in the corner, and breaking it open seized a long uncut piece of the home-spun, and trailing it proudly behind him boasted: "Make Indian good shirt!" This was more than could be endured by the woman who had spun and woven it with

DOG'S HOLE, PALENVILLE.

her own hands, and making a dash at the impious red man, Vrouw Scrope shouted: "You no hef dat! dat Bastyon's piece!"

Old Mr. Scrope coming in at this juncture was filled with horror at his wife's rashness and cried: "Vor Cot's sake, let dem hef vat dey vill, you lose your het yet!" But the warning proved of no avail, for what was a Dutch vrouw's life worth to her despoiled of her store of linen, and the Indian soon settled the point by killing the brave woman and laying her husband dead beside her. The daughter, while this scene was being enacted and all the Indians intent upon the issue, quickly snatched her baby from the bed, and gathering her three other children together, fled with them through a back door and hid with them in a field of rye.

The Indians soon fired the house and left, bearing with them much plunder, including, no doubt, " Bastyon's piece," so valiantly defended, and the boy Schermerhorn as a captive.

At their departure the terrified young mother crept from her hiding-place, and with her little ones followed the Kiskatom creek to the house of Mr. Timmerman, five miles away. Meanwhile the husband, Schermerhorn, returned from his two days' journey to mill, and found his home in ashes, with no trace of its inmates but a few charred bones. Half crazed with grief at the possible fate of his family, he at last found his wife and children and learned from them the death of his parents and the captivity of his younger brother. He quickly formed a party of men and went in pursuit of the savages, but as well pursue the east wind, for their path over the mountains was as trackless.

The story of the long march, the days of hunger and parching thirst, through the summer heat, the weary feet bleeding and sore, and yet the lips not daring to complain lest the tomahawk should quickly settle all, makes a sad history indeed.

One night, encamped near Schoharie, the Indians drew forth the scalps of the murdered Scropes and proceeded to dry them on little hoops before the fire. One of the men, making a third hoop, suddenly sprung up with a savage yell and made a dash at Schermerhorn, who now stood transfixed with fright. Seizing the boy by the hair, he made passes at him with the scalping-knife, when the poor youth could endure no more and fell fainting with terror and exhaustion at his captor's feet. The other Indians, immensely diverted by this witty sally on the part of their companion, rolled over and over on the ground screaming with laughter. On another occasion the lad was made to " run the gauntlet," a hideous custom rigidly adhered to by all Indians bearing away captives. When approaching a settlement of friendly savages, the prisoner was stripped naked and compelled to pass between two lines of the villagers, whose custom was to shower on the victim all kinds of torments in the shape of blows, pricks, and cuts from sharp knives. Lucky was the man who came through the ordeal alive.

At Fort Niagara—Ne-a-*gaa*-ra the Indians called it always—Schermerhorn's captors received eight dollars apiece for the scalps they brought, that being the usual bounty paid by the British for such rebel head-gear, and forty dollars for their prisoner, who was forthwith impressed into the army. From that time he saw no more of home or friends till the year after the close of the war, when he wandered back and at last found his parents living in Hudson.

Along the line of the Hudson River, about half a mile from its west bank, runs a line of abruptly rising hills, called " The Collaberg." Near Catskill they dip suddenly to the westward into a narrow valley, across which hills rise again in higher crests toward the mountains. Where Kaaterskill creek comes winding down from its birthplace in the Catskills, and crosses this lovely little valley, there spreads out a plateau of fertile farm-land. There, in a sheltered spot, by a glassy pool, where willows dip and swing to their long reflections in the water, and swallows go darting in and out through the long summer afternoons, the Abiel family had reared a home that was more like a rude fortress for their household gods. The house is of stone, as the houses of the prosperous Dutch were in those times, low and wide-spreading, with small windows, easily defended, and a great oaken house-door divided across midway.

One evening, in the spring of 1781, the cows were chewing peaceful cuds in the farm-yard, the hens were on the roost, and all things outside had a " ready-for-bed " aspect, while within the family were seated at supper. The Dutch were a silent folk, and the Abiels were no exception to the rule, so that the picture of the supper, viewed through the open upper half of the great door, was that of a noiseless, pantomimic feast. Was it a real scene, or only a vision ? Evidently the spectators, lurking without, determined to try what stuff it might be made of, for suddenly a terrific war-whoop filled all the quiet place with unearthly clamor. The family spang up as one man, so schooled were they to expect danger, and reached for the guns kept loaded and resting on brackets attached to the huge beams overhead. But it was too late, and before a blow could be struck they were surrounded by a band of Mohawks. The treacherous slaves of the household either slunk away in hiding or aided the Indians in securing the captives. The woman and children were not molested, nor would David Abiel have been taken, but for his incautious exclamation on recognizing one of his Tory neighbors in his disguise of an Indian, and crying aloud in his indignation : " What, is dat you ! "

Long years after, a sister of David Abiel was fond of relating the story of the seizure, and how she had retained her presence of mind sufficiently to slip under the table and take off the men's shoe- and knee-buckles, anticipating their probable captivity ! No climax of life or death could engross the Knickerbocker mind to the exclusion of thrift.

Garrett Abiel, one of the younger sons, had been absent during the day at Domine Schunneman's, and, returning in the evening, heard the noises in the house and immediately understood

what had happened. Hurrying away, he secured the help of a
near neighbor, and, returning, hid in the bushes near the barn.
As the savages passed out with their captives, young Abiel raised
his gun to shoot, but the neighbor stopped him, saying : " You
might kill your own father ! "

So the party passed along unhindered, to the rendezvous at Pine
Orchard on the mountains. Here they encamped, for Brant was in-
festing the mountains, preparing for a general descent upon the valley ; meanwhile, parties were sent out here and there for Whig captives. Old David Abiel's reputation for patriotism, or attachment
to the cause of " rebellion," was as great as his fame for honesty and
bravery, so that he was, upon the whole, valuable, though too old
now for a soldier. So well was his character for probity recognized, that some of his Tory neighbors in disguise, consorting
with Brant's men, induced the savages to put him on parole, thinking that the surest way to prevent him from making his escape.
At the close of their stay on the mountains, a large party of Whigs
from the valley made an attack, with the purpose of rescuing the
captives. Successful in the case of some of the victims, they failed
to rescue the Abiels, because of this very parole of the old man's.
Left in the rear of the departing Indians, they found the old man
plodding doggedly along after his red-skinned enemies, and
called upon him loudly to stop and turn about in his march.

" But no ! " cried the honest Dutchman, whose brain was incapable of entertaining more subtle distinctions of morality than
just abstract right and wrong, " I hef given my word to the sal-
vages, end I must go with them ! "

Then there was a great time made over his obstinacy, and
his duty held up before him in various guises. He was finally
conjured, for the sake of his wife and children, to return and protect them and their home. Still the old man was unmoved, stand-

ing squarely and half defiantly, lest any one, more bold than the others, should lay hold of him and force him back to his home, and yet the tears were rolling down his honest cheeks as even his naturally unimaginative mind portrayed for him the trials and privations, perhaps even the death, that awaited him on the long westward march ; and, on the other hand, the welcome home where were his wife and loving children to soothe the cares of coming years. It was a hard thing for these good neighbors to fight, at risk of life, for the liberty of a man who would not take it when it came, but only said, staunchly, as if defending his honor : " Want wat baat het een mensch zoo hij de gehule wereld gewint, en lijdt schade zijner zeile. Of wot zal een mensch geren, tot lossing van zijne zeile ! " These are the words of Matthew : " What shall it profit a man if he gain the whole world and lose his soul ? "

The domine came up at this pass, and hearing the state of things gazed on his parishioner with a sorrowful heart, saying : " I am sorry ; and I am rejoiced. Such honor is seen but in the true-hearted and God shall reward it—our good Dutch Church is represented in you this day, and the fame thereof will go far among the Gentiles," then the good old man lifted up his voice in prayer, ending with the solemn apostolic benediction in Dutch : " De genade onzes Heeven Jesus Christus zij met uwen geest ! Amen." And Elder Abiel turned back to trace the weary road to his captivity.

There are many versions of this captivity, one as authentic as another, perhaps, but I choose this one with its noble picture of the old Dutchman whose simple heart was incapable of a broken promise, choosing hardship and pain—perhaps death itself—with the consciousness of an unsullied honor, rather than home and love and the peaceful joys of declining years, purchased with a violated parole. Bless his old heart! I can see him yet, with his short, bandy legs clad in long hose and short trunks, with his broad back and big hat, trudging honestly over the trail toward Hunter. And yet there is, of course, an element of absurdity in it all too. Did so simple a device as carrying him off home whether or no never occur to the simple Boermen? Surely they could so have saved his honor and his sacrifice at once.

The rage and disgust of his son Anthony must have been great next morning, when the old man walked into the Indian camp by Schoharie Kill and gave himself up.

Having spoken to the leader in the Indian tongue, Elder Abiel was asked where he learned that language. Receiving in reply the answer that he had formerly been a trader among the Mohawks, they treated him with some kindness during the remainder of his journey. His son Anthony was obliged to run the gauntlet more than once, and at the best showing they had enough of hunger and fatigue and every hardship to endure.

On reaching the fort at Niagara, David Abiel was soon released on account of his age, but Anthony was kept for two years longer in a vain attempt to force him into the British service, when he escaped with the Snyders, an account of whose captivity is found below.

About a mile north of the Blue Mountain Dutch Church, which stands on a breezy hill-top, face to face with the panorama of the Catskills, on a farm now in possession of the Valks, stands the ruin of Captain Elias Snyder's homestead. Seemingly alone and deserted now, it is yet haunted by ghostly memories that figure in long by-gone dramas. To one of a sensitive fancy it is an evil place of a dark night. I am told that it is no uncommon occurrence for the old rooms to be once more lighted up with tallow-dips and for the bright fire of logs to be kindled again in the great cavern of a fireplace. Then the broad Dutch lasses with their long braids hanging from under the closely-tied caps, their quilted petticoats balancing with the rigidity of big bells of brass, go swinging down the centre of a reel, hand-in-hand with their "Garretjes" and "Jacobs" and "Tjerks," whose breadth of beam in their duck-tail coats, brave in huge buttons, is something marvellous to behold. Sometimes it is a *pas-seul* which some awkward gallant executes under the festoons of dried apples and red peppers that hang from the beams.

The fun grows more excited, the lights flare up and *gros-muder* is seen through the window preparing to open the little door of the big oven beside the fireplace.

She is old and wrinkled, with a baleful light in her wicked eye, as she leans with her long-handled shovel on which to slide out the goodies baking in there. She lifts the latch when—puff! A great blaze leaps out and devours her bodily before your eyes, and not only her but the dancers, the dried apples, the red peppers, and all in a fiery cauldron! The moon has risen behind the old house and now it shines, a great red ball, through sash-less windows and sill-less door-ways. And yet they say it is not all an illusion of the moonlight—but to my story.

The Snyders were wood-choppers, and yet the father of the family was also captain of militia, such were the mixed conditions of this primitive life. As an officer of the rebels this captive was a prize coveted by his Tory neighbors, since the reward given for him, dead or alive, would be high. His danger was great as his daily work led him away in the forest, sometimes quite alone, and sometimes accompanied only by his son, Elias. One day they were startled, while at work, by perceiving two parties of Tories and Indians coming upon them from opposite directions. Dropping their axes they ran wildly toward home, closely pursued by the enemy.

75   PROFILE ROCK.

Among the Indians were two men well known to the settlers as "John Rump" and "Hank's Ben." Nearing the house, the Snyders found themselves cut off from safety there by another party coming to meet them, so they stopped running and gave up. Captain Snyder felt himself fortunate to get off with his life and only a scalp wound, even though he must go into captivity.

The savages now proceeded to the house, from which the women and children had fled to the woods, and rifled it of clothing, provisions, and money. Dividing the booty into packs, the captors led the road, over which so many weary feet had passed to Canada, or perished by the way.

Winding up the "clove" in the mountain the trail was a pathway fit for fairy travellers. A carpet of soft gray and green moss, with now and then a patch of the graceful partridge-berry, that prettiest of ground-runners, or the nodding plumes of princes-feather, or the rich red-splashed leaves of the liver-wort, while overhead arched whispering birches, whose white trunks gleamed through the twilight of the forest like the robes of slim maidens clad in bridal garments. Now and then a rustle, or a darting form, gave hint of the wild pulsing life hidden in the heart of the groves whose privacy these stealthy, murderous steps were invading. But these lovely and delicate forms had no attraction for those, who leaving home and friends for a long foot-journey filled with danger and suffering, could think only of the simple joys and home-peace left behind, and the torture and death that might lurk ahead.

Taking an oblique path across the mountains they passed through Palenville clove, and there one of the Indians climbed upon a ledge near Profile Rock to look back over the valley before proceeding farther. His two captives clambered up after him, and here it was that, hidden by a projecting rock from the savages below, Elias Snyder would have killed him, but the more prudent father restrained his son, and thus one chance of liberty passed by, and the Indian never guessed his danger. From here they went southward across Pine Orchard near where the Laurel House now stands, and so over between the two lakes to the Schoharie Kill, which they waded breast high, walking on ten miles farther without changing their clothes. At the head of the Schoharie Kill, in a ravine, was kept a store of corn for the wants of the tribe as they went back and forth on these long marches, and their hunting expeditions. Here they supplied themselves, and here it was that " my poy, Elias," gave evidence of his Dutch shrewdness. Finding his share of the burden too heavy to suit him he began complimenting one of the braves on his great strength, whereupon the besetting vanity of the Indian induced him to transfer the larger part of Elias' corn to his own pack and carry it away on his proud shoulders. Coming to the Genesee River they met there a white woman of about twenty-five years of age, in Indian dress, and carrying in her arms a baby in whose face the Indian and white blood were traceable. Beside her was her husband, a Seneca chief. She asked the Snyders many questions about their homes and people, telling them that she had been taken captive in the old French war and the Indians had brought her up as one of themselves. She knew nothing now of her people or their fate, and said that she felt no desire to return to the whites. They were much struck by her beauty and intelligence.

A funny example of the Indian taciturnity, or perhaps his idea of courtesy, is given by Rockwell in his "Catskill Mountains." He says : " The Indian who tomahawked Captain Snyder shaved him twice a week but never spoke of, nor seemed to notice the wounds on his head.

The Snyders after their arrival at Niagara were sent to Montreal, where they were closely questioned by the British officers, and then assigned to a filthy and crowded prison called the " Berot." Their food was stinted and of poor quality, they were infested with vermin, and, to add to their suffering, they were treated with great inhumanity by the Hessian guards. They often heard in Montreal the yell customary on entering the town with scalps, and saw from their prison windows the hideous trophies carried by in triumph, strung on long poles.

After a while the Snyders, and the Abiels of Catskill, who had come hither during the previous year, were billeted on parole among the Canadians of the little island of Jésu, farther up the river. Rockwell mentions as one of the hardships they had here to endure, that " the women were many and ill-natured, and tried to prevent their making tea ! "

In August, 1782, Captain Abiel was sent home under escort, being over fifty, and hence not formidable as an active enemy, nor useful as an impressed soldier. It was only the scalps of the old men, and of women and children, that were of value.

Here our captives lived in the little settlement for some months in comparative peace, despite the numerous and anti-tea women, and now they began to lay plans for another escape. And many a careful parley was necessary to undertake so hazardous an enterprise, for even supposing they could pass the argus eyes of their watchful enemies, there lay before them the march of several hundred miles through a trackless wilderness without a guide ; and of necessity, with no provision for their hunger other than the watchful care of Him who cares for the sparrows. One obstacle to their plans lay in the impossibility of convincing Captain Snyder that his parole was a matter of no binding character. Argue as they would, he came back always to the one point—a man's word is his oath, and there was an end of the matter. A Dutchman's word of honor in those days was as great a security as iron chains. At last, however, the conditions of the parole were thoughtlessly broken in some way not given, by the officers themselves, and the scrupulous Hollander felt himself released from the bond.

The party obtained, without difficulty, a passport to Montreal, where they purchased as great curiosities, pretending ignorance of their use, three pocket compasses. The Fourth of July being at hand they provided themselves with four gallons of wine, says my trusty chronicler, two of rum, and sufficient loaf-sugar to sweeten this most ungodly drink, and then they set themselves about the work of "celebration." We are not told that the Abiels and Snyders, now three in all, consumed this amount unaided, but I am unable to find any trace of more members of the celebrating party.

The 10th of September was the day finally fixed upon for escape ; accordingly, while the Canadian family upon whom they were quartered were at supper, the Snyders procured three loaves of bread and some pork from the cellar, secreting them in a convenient place. While vespers were in progress, they stole away, and joining the younger Abiel and a Chas. Butler, of Philadelphia, started for the lower end of the island. The night was stormy and dark, and the river swollen and very rough, but they finished that portion of the perilous journey in safety, landing several miles down the river. In a day or two they began the long march homeward, coming soon upon an encampment of Indians, whom they avoided just in time to escape a second capture. The greatest danger soon threatened them, for the bread now gave out and the awful problem of providing sustenance by the way appeared for solution. However, they pressed on, trusting to find something to stay the pangs of hunger. In any event it were better to die in a determined effort to reach home and the duties that called so loudly for their presence, than to lie pent up on the little island while their neighbors and friends were fighting for liberty.

After four days of hunger they found spignet root and lived on that till they reached the Connecticut River. Here, by the riverside, by a deserted camp-fire, " my poy Elias," ever lucky and thrifty, found the thigh-bone of a moose, the remnant of some hunter's feast. Nothing remained but the sinews and bone, but he burned it and, powdering it, lived on it for three days. Soon they succeeded in their efforts to catch trout in the river, and then the supply of rations began to improve. They concluded to cross the river, and Elias, attempting to swim it, narrowly escaped drowning, for, exhausted by fasting and fatigue, he sunk under the light burden of his pack, but making one vigorous effort gained shallower water and waded ashore.

" Not far from this point "—I quote from Rockwell—" they found the first traces of civilized inhabitants. They ate blackberries, in a new field covered with them, and some two miles beyond came to a log-house, the owner of which was working in a field. Captain Snyder and Abiel went toward him to inquire for provisions, while the others entered the cabin and helped themselves to part of a loaf of bread, which was all the provisions the poor man had. The same evening they went about a mile farther, to the house of a man named Williams, whose family kindly gave up to them their supper of hasty-pudding and moose pie. Here, they remained all night, and in the morning several of the neighbors came in with a magistrate named Ames, who, after examining them, furnished Captain Snyder with a passport for himself and his comrades to the head-quarters of General Bailey, at the lower Coos. They were now in New Hampshire, among a very humane and generous people, who liberally supplied their wants. But such was their appetite, after enduring extreme hunger, that they commonly ate six meals a day of light food, and thus made small progress. Sunday, September 29th, they reached General Bailey's quarters, who received them with great kindness. He ordered shoes to be made and mended for them ; and there they remained two days, when Captain Snyder, having been furnished with a horse by the General, left his companions, and returned home through Massachusetts and Connecticut, crossing the Hudson River at Poughkeepsie. The others went by way of Sunderland and Pittsfield, Massachusetts, and crossed the river near Kinderhook. Captain Snyder reached home first, where he found his relatives living and in good health. The joy of their meeting we need not attempt to describe."

So ends the story of this captivity in Canada, but not the list of those who suffered in like manner. There were many others whose names we come upon here and there in dusty old chronicles, and many more whose names we know not, whose unnoticed, insignificant lives slipped away in the shade, and ended in wigwams, long years after, in the far-away wilderness. Many women and little children were taken, and very few of these ever reached Canada and the British. The braves took them for themselves, and the mothers wore away their darkened days carrying burdens, working the soil to raise corn and lentils, and bearing children to their loathed captors. Happy was she whose child was left to her then, at any price, for oftener the little one and its mother found homes far asunder.

One account of a capture by the Indians is very touching in its simple pathos. Among the Huguenots who settled near Kingston in those early days was Louis Dubois and his wife, Catharine Lefever Dubois, and three children. The wife and children were carried off with some other persons in one of the frequents attacks of unfriendly savages. The distracted husband sought for them

in vain, and at last, as all hope of ever finding his dear ones
had left him, he one day received a visit from an Indian to whom
he had once done a kindness. The Indian told him that by following the course of the Rondout, and then Wallkill Creek, branching
off again along the course of a smaller tributary, the captives could
be found in an Indian camp. It is worthy of note here, that
the spot indicated was about one hundred yards east of the
Shawangunk Creek, at a point very near where the Shawangunk
Dutch Church now stands.

Thus advised, Dubois immediately started with a small party of
men, with dogs, guns, and provisions, marching through the forest
twenty-six miles to the appointed place.

Before reaching the camp they met an Indian who wellnigh
put a stop to the expedition by shooting at Dubois, but fortunately
the arrow missed its mark, and Dubois, falling on the savage, killed
him with his sword before the other Indians were warned of the
approach of the rescuing party.

Proceeding now with the greatest care, they came to a place
where they could look down from a slight eminence on the camp,
where a remarkable scene met their eyes. The Indians were preparing to march westward, and had decided to kill their captives,
thus obviating the necessity of feeding them on the journey. The
wretched women and children were tied to trees, while about
them were piled dried sticks and leaves showing the fiendish purpose of burning them alive.

Mrs. Dubois, however, being a woman of great piety and faith,
and possessed withal, of a marvellously sweet and powerful voice,
say the old chronicles, in the midst of these preparations, began to
sing, partly to encourage, perhaps, her terrified little ones, and also
to sustain her own soul through this dreadful ordeal. The song
that rose to her lips was a paraphrase of that beautiful psalm,

descriptive of the captive Jews by the rivers of Babylon, as with harps hung on the willows they sat them down and wept. The Indians, unused to such sweet music and attracted by the song, when she had finished came crowding around her, bidding her sing again, and this was the scene that met the eyes of her husband and friends as they came stealing through the undergrowth. The captive with arms tied behind her, her lovely face lifted to heaven, was singing with all her soul mounting upward through her wonderful voice, while the savages stood about her, transfixed with delight, and the children and two neighbor women who were tied to trees near by were listening to the holy words, their faces, all tear-stained, taking on new courage.

CLIMBING UP, PALENVILLE OVERLOOK.

Suddenly one of the dogs that accompanied the searchers set up a howl and startled the savages, while they, thinking a large party of unfriendly men were upon them, were immediately on the alert. There was nothing for it now but prompt action on the part of Dubois and his men, for the Indians far outnumbered them, so they set up a great shouting and hallooing before making their appearance, as if twice their number were there, and the savages immediately rushed off to save themselves in the wilderness. Cutting hastily the cords that bound the captives, they dashed away, and the poor frightened wretches fancying themselves surprised by other savages dashed after their cruel captors in a panic. Dubois, however, soon overtook his wife and children, and great indeed was the joy of that deliverance. The poor woman's stout heart gave out at last, and she swooned away in her husband's arms.

She came back to her home and friends, with herself and the little ones unharmed, but her face, still young and fair, was from that time framed in white locks instead of brown, and till her death, many years after, she carried, as a badge of her awful suspense and suffering, her long, wavy hair turned snowy white.

The dinner-bell somewhat damaged the effect of the last sentence, but each hastened to make a kind criticism on the Captain's stories; even Miss Polly was somewhat melted.

Coming out of the dining-room, a burst of sunshine on the veranda caused universal rejoicing. There was a rush for hats and walking-sticks, the more prudent securing umbrellas, and the usual hegira took place. Troops of laughing girls and a few dapper youths went to the tennis ground, the children to the swings and croquet, while the stout dowagers took possession of the veranda, sending even the babies with their nurses out into the delicious air. The energetic Miss Perkins started out to explore the little village accompanied by John Grant, whom nothing less than the attractions of so bright and pretty a girl would have tempted from a lazy afternoon under the trees in a hammock ; for he fitted well the old descriptive doggerel, " long and lazy."

Many a pretty bit of rock and glen rewarded them, however, for taking to the bank of the stream, a course always productive of good results in a hilly country. They followed it upward, on beyond the old mill, past a charming house that rumor says was made out of a barn, and so along by waterfalls and miniature rapids till well up the mountain they sat down to rest near where a bridge crosses the chasm, under the shadow of a great rock. The climb had made them very warm, and the shade was proportionately grateful. Miss Polly leaned back against the rock and listened to the voice of her comrade, as it mingled with the tinkle and murmur of the stream, till she began to think the talk was getting rather personal. Suddenly her eyes were fixed on the rocks beyond and above them, and she cried out :

" Oh, stop, please ! There is an eavesdropper, and a most uncanny one too ! "

Above them leaned a giant face cut in the rock, as if by the cunning chisel of man. The Literary Fellow readily recognized it as being the well-known " Profile Rock," and congratulated Miss Polly on their narrow escape from passing it unnoticed.

" He looks as if set here to guard some treasure,—you know there is endless gold in these hills."

" Then let 's go instantly and begin looking for some ! "

So saying, the indefatigable maiden sprung up, and they continued their upward walk.

Gold has been found, and, perhaps, silver, at various times in the Catskills, but no success seems to attend its removal ; and, indeed, it has seemed almost impossible to find a second time the lucky spot. The Indians believed that the Great Spirit, who had a home in these hills, was displeased at any search for gold here, and would ever lay obstacles in the way of its removal. The first knowledge of its presence here, by the whites, was on an occasion of a peace parley between Wilhemus Kieft, Director of the New Netherlands, and a band of Mohawk chiefs. Kieft was accompanied by Mynheer Adrian Van der Donk, his learned friend, and they both noticed a pigment that one of the chiefs used in decorating himself, and were struck with its weight and shining yellow appearance. They procured a lump and took it back with them to New Amsterdam (New York), where it was assayed, and yielded gold to about the value of three guilders. Overjoyed at this discovery, our discreet Dutch friends kept it a profound secret. They sent a party of men back to the Mohawks, who furnished them with a guide, and the result of this expedition was a bucketful of ore, equally productive of the precious metal. The chiefs looked very gloomy at this spoliation of their god's territory, and predicted that no good would come of it. Kieft, however, sent a trusty messenger—Arent Corsen—to Holland, with a bagful of the gold, as a welcome token to the home Government of the heretofore unexpected richness of this New-World plantation.

Corson embarked, about Christmas, on an English ship, intending to cross afterward to Rotterdam, but the vessel was wrecked, and all on board perished. Thus Manitou punished their cupidity. In 1647, when Petrus Stuyvesant took charge of New Netherland, Kieft embarked for Holland, carrying another sackful of the Catskill ore, but that, too, proved a Jonah, and all on board this ship went to the bottom with the treasure.

A few years afterward, Mynheer Brant Arent Van Schlechtenhorst, agent for the Patroon of Renselaerwyck, purchased for the Patroon, a tract of land on the mountains, and leased it in farms. A young Dutch girl, daughter of one of these farmers, found, one day, in her rambles on the mountains, a piece of some white, shining substance, which was immediately supposed to be silver, and sent to Van Schlechtenhorst. He dispatched his son post-haste to investigate the matter, and the young man arrived at the close of an autumn day at the farmer's house. The evening he devoted to looking about the place, being much struck by the beauty of the situation the farmer had chosen for his home, beside a tinkling little mountain stream. In the night, however, this little stream rose to a great flood, the rain fell in torrents, and the heavens were rent with the fury of the storm. The house went floating down the stream, and the young Van Schlechtenhorst barely escaped with his life. As soon as possible he returned home, saying that nothing would induce him again to brave the spirit of those enchanted hills, who was evidently determined that none should find his hoarded treasure.

Soon after these events, a great quarrel arose between the doughty Petrus Stuyvesant and the haughty Patroon Van Renselaer, and the Patroon's agent was thrown into prison at New Amsterdam. This abode must have chilled his adventurous spirit and quenched his thirst for gold, for we hear no more of his attempts, in the dispute that followed about the right to the Catskill lands.

Some of the treasure brought to the port of New York under the rule of the English Col. Fletcher, when so many pirates were said to have been harbored in that wicked city, was buried, says tradition, on the shores of the Hudson, and much was secreted in the Catskills, whether buried or hidden in its numerous caves is left untold. Certain it is that Captain Kidd, one of the boldest and most successful of these pirates, is known to have taken a journey into the mountains, on his return from one rich expedition, and some important business connected with his plunder must have carried him there. Therefore we see clearly that John Grant's tale of Kidd's adventure here must have the best of claims to be set down with Captain Oldbore's authenticated facts.

On South Mountain Miss Polly was much impressed with the huge boulders of pudding-stone that lie scattered about there as if they had rained down from above. Having expressed that idea she was startled by the reply, "and so they did," from the Literary Fellow.

"Oh! I see you do not believe me. Well, it is an Indian legend with whatever value you choose to put upon it."

So he told her the story of the Stone Giants.

These dread foes were said to be descended from a family near the Mississippi, and wandering away in the wilderness they forgot in their sufferings that they were men. Like beasts, they devoured the flesh of men when they found a man to kill. They so hardened the skin of their bodies by various practices, among which was rolling in the sand, that the arrows of the Iroquois rattled in vain on their toughened hides. They fought many successful battles against their enemies, and pressed forward to the Catskills. Here they lived for a time in caves, descending upon the tribes about the region of Stony Clove and Windham, as those parts are now called, and carrying away captives, to devour alive in their caves about South Mountain and Overlook. At last the great Manitou became exasperated, and finding that his children could not drive them out unaided, went himself against them. In the disguise of a giant he marshalled them as leader, brandishing a huge club, and led them forth to find their enemies. Through all the winding paths of the mountains he led them a day's journey, bringing them, all unsuspecting, to his own South Mountain,—some versions have it Indian Head,—and there in the darkness he made great rocks to fall from heaven and crush them. Unto this day, there lie the great boulders of pudding-stone, as their monuments. It would be a fine corroboration to roll one down the mountain side and find the remains of a fierce demon beneath!

Early in the morning of the following day the party were once more on the march. A carriage-drive brought them to the station at Haines' Corners, and here presently came the snorting little fiend of an engine to drag its freight of passengers through the strongholds of the great Manitou. What a desecrating thought! No wonder the heavens are frowning and the mountain sides seem to threaten instant destruction, as they speed away under the shadows !

VIEWS IN STONY CLOVE.

At Tannersville Junction they left the train and walked through the "Notch." Two colossal walls of stone towered high on either side, and an icy chill struck to the marrow as they passed between. A spell seemed on the place, and no one spoke a word. Mrs. Schuyler drew her shawl more closely about her and shivered, while every one looked apprehensively up from time to time as if expecting the great rocks to close in, crushing these audacious intruders. On the way a great black pool opened to view, reflecting in its depths the frowning masses above. The ef-

GLOOMY POOL BEYOND THE NOTCH.

fect was weird, and Miss Rutherford murmured : " Poe should have seen and immortalized this spot."

At Edgewood the party regained its spirits. The sun came out illuminating between soft clouds the panorama that unfolds itself there. The northern view is bounded by the two mountains forming the Notch, but far away southward the hills roll away like the receding waves of a vast ocean.

Through the fine farming country to Phœnicia, they then go by the train again, and thence westward to Dry Brook valley and

FARM-HOUSES NEAR PHŒNICIA.

the head waters of the Delaware. They felt they could not miss a glimpse, even if it must be from the window of a railroad train, of so lovely a country as that. Back again now to West Hurley, and there they take mountain wagons for Overlook. Not one of them all was loath to lie down that night, and sleep as only the care-free or the thoroughly weary ever do sleep.

The Overlook is that part of the mountain where the early Dutch settlers believed that Hendrick Hudson kept vigil over his loved river, and it is on the cliff near the house where

Cooper places Natty Bumpo when he looked forth and saw
"all creation."

"'I have travelled the woods for fifty-three years,'" said Leath-
er-Stocking, "'and have made them my home for more than
forty : and I can say that I have met but one place that was more
to my liking ; and that was only to eyesight, and not for hunting
or fishing.'"

"'And where was that?'" asked Edwards.

"'Where! why, up on the Catskills. I used often to go up
into the mountains after wolves' skins and bears ; once they
brought me to get them a stuffed painter ; and so I often went.
There 's a place in them hills that I used to climb to when I
wanted to see the carryings on of the world, that would well pay
any man for a barked shin or a torn moccasin. You know the
Catskills, lad, for you must have seen them on your left as you
followed the river up from York, looking as blue as a piece
of clear sky, and holding the clouds on their tops, as the smoke
curls over the head of an Indian chief at a council fire. Well,
there 's the High-peak and the Round-top, which lay back, like a
father and mother among their children, seeing they are far above
all the other hills. But the place I mean is next to the river,
where one of the ridges juts out a little from the rest, and where
the rocks fall for the best part of a thousand feet so much up and
down that a man standing on their edges is fool enough to think
he can jump from top to bottom.'"

"'What see you when you get there?'" asked Edwards.

"'Creation!'" said Natty, dropping the end of his rod into the
water, and sweeping one hand around him in a circle, '"all creation,
lad. I was on that hill when Vaughan burnt Sopus, in the last
war ; and I seen the vessels come out of the Highlands as plainly
as I can see that lime-scow rowing into the Susquehanna, though

one was twenty times farther from me than the other. The river was in sight for seventy miles under my feet, looking like a curled shaving, though it was eight long miles to its bank. I saw the hills in the Hampshire grants, the highlands of the river, and all that God had done or man could do, as far as the eye could reach, — you know that the Indians named me for my sight, lad, —and, from the flat on the top of that mountain, I have often found the place where Albany stands ; and, as for Sopus, the day the royal troops burned the town the smoke seemed so nigh that I thought I could hear the screeches of the women.' "

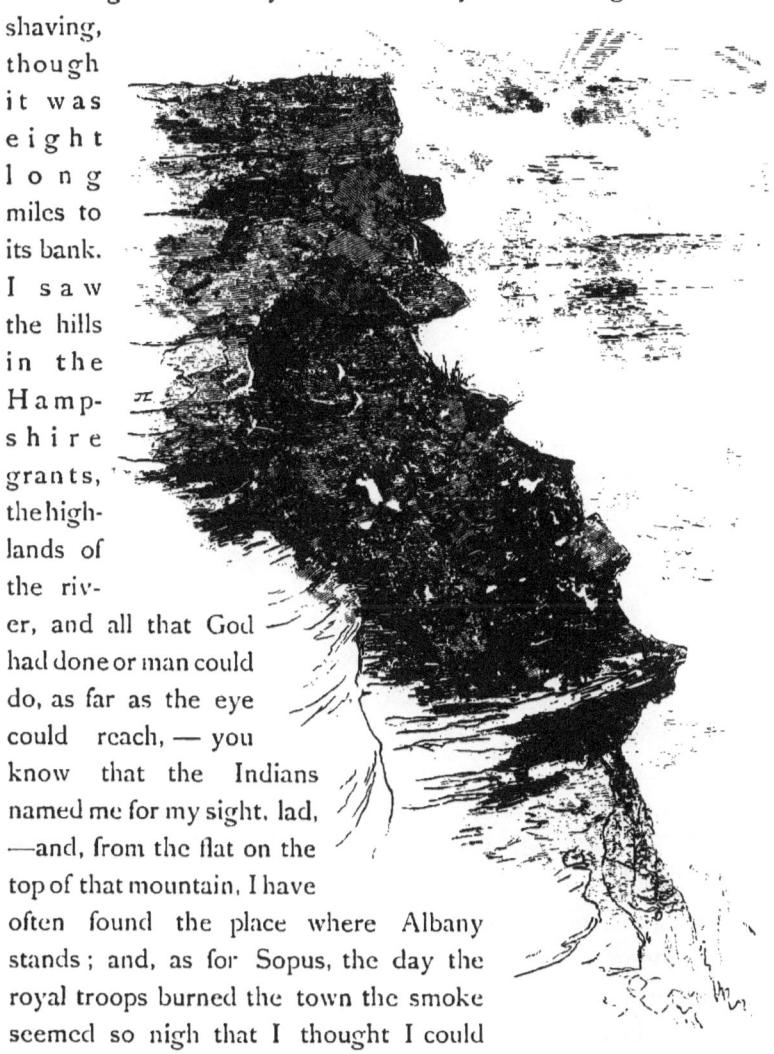

DOMINIE'S FACE.

" ' It must have been worth the toil to meet with such a glorious view.' "

" ' If being the best part of a mile in the air, and having men's farms and houses at your feet, with rivers looking like ribbands, and mountains bigger than the " vision " seeming to be haystacks of green grass under you, gives any satisfaction to a man, I recommend the spot ! ' "

So it was that when our pilgrims came to see the attractions of

ECHO LAKE.

Overlook and its views, that all its associations came up, first suggested by one, then by another, until even Captain Oldbore waxed eloquent over the burning of Esopus as it lay to the south of them.

At Echo Lake they were impressed with a certain air of mystery that seemed to permeate the place, and John Grant promised them a legend concerning it to be told that night in the moonlight, over in the grove near the tower.

Here it was, by the lake-side, that they fell in with old Stubble, the mountain seer. For so many years that the memory of man seems to run not to the contrary, he has presided as a sort of divinity over these mountains. Indeed, by his own " cackleation "

—as he calls it—he must be fully two hundred years old, though the ordinary observer would hardly give him more than sixty winters. He is renowned for his shrewd wit, his accurate knowledge of the Catskills, and his highly apocryphal yarns. As for the latter, it would be a hardy man indeed who would dare to correct his stories the second time. If you would enjoy him to the full, you must take him at his own valuation and listen respectfully. He took a sudden fancy to Miss Rutherford, and when the plan of walking back to the hotel through the woods was proposed, he hitched up his butternut overalls, expectorated with great dexterity at the knot of a young birch-tree trunk a few yards distant, and spoke :

" Naow ef ye say so, I 'll jest pilot ye up that mounting thoo the woods, an' 't ain't no sich easy thing ez you think neither, ef the path *is* blazed, which them blazes is all growed over 'bout."

Half way up he stopped to " blow ye," he said, and resting one foot on a fallen tree and leaning his arm on the bent knee, asked, " Ben to the falls in the Plattekill I sposin ? "

On being informed that although they had not, they fully intended doing so, he announced with perfect simplicity :

" Them falls useter run tother way. I recklect it puffectly well. All that water run west inter the Schoharie Kill."

Every one seemed struck speechless by this stupendous lie save Miss Rutherford, and her social tact came to fill the significant silence.

" Indeed, that 's an interesting thing to remember ! "

" Aint it, now ? " he continued, evidently pleased by her ready credence. " Yaas, that was the spring I got word from my brother in West Constant, saying he 's sick, and wantin' me to come on. But takes a sight 'o money to git thet fur, and a body hez to begin to cumerlate (accumulate) long afore—so I coulden' go, but that 's the year, nigh bout fifty year ago I guess, that the water in that thar stream turned en begun to run tother way."

After some reflection most of the party seemed to look on this as a masterpiece, the Literary Fellow especially seemed to admire Stubble's talent, and nothing less than taking the old man up to the hotel to dine would satisfy him.

That evening by the fitful light of the moon, as clouds now and then darkened its disc, only to pass and let all its radiance down into the valley, the story of Echo Lake was told.

HAIDONI AND THE VAMPYRES.

" Haidoni was a hero of great fame among the six nations and the Seneca tribe. So great was his bravery and his pride in showing it, that Manitou was especially favorable to him, and helped him through many of his difficult exploits. Not the least of these had been an excursion alone to the Cher-okees in search of scalps and glory. The Iroquois counted life well lost for the latter achievement. Taking nothing for his long journey to the Western plains but his bow and arrows, and a little pouchful of parched and ground corn, which has great sustaining qualities, he set out. After long wandering with many remarkable experiences, and escapes from death, he came to a Cherokee council fire. The council broke up in a dance, and soon one of the young

VAMPYRE'S DEN, AND
DEATH OF STONE GIANT.

braves wandering into the bushes, our hero quickly despatched him without noise and secured his scalp. He got three similar trophies in this manner and then left, stealing away through the undergrowth to escape detection. On his homeward journey, he came to a lodge in a lonely place, and waiting here in the same manner as before, soon secured the life and scalp of its owner. Entering the lodge in search of plunder he found food and tobacco, having enjoyed which, he lay down on the bed in the corner, and soon fell asleep. He was awakened by the entrance of an old squaw, who, mistaking him for her murdered son, said: " My son, I am going away, and will not be back till to-morrow." When she had left him, he sprang up, and, hastily appropriating what food could be found, fled. And none too soon was his flight begun, for his inroads having been traced he was hotly pursued, and barely escaped, to tell the tale of his prowess, and display his four scalps about the friendly fires of his own people.

Haidoni's favorite employment was hunting deer, and his customary hunting-ground the lake behind Overlook Mountain. Here, on dark nights, he would paddle noiselessly in his bark canoe, hidden by green boughs in front of him, and with a flaring pine knot fastened at the prow. The timid creatures, attracted by the light, would come to the water's edge, when a noiseless arrow speeding on its unerring errand of death finished the story. Sometimes as many fine bucks as the fingers on both his hands, he was said to have killed thus in a night. But one night, as he stole along seeking here and there for the shadow on the shore, and the two bright dazzled eyes that indicated his prey, his usual good genius seemed to have deserted him, for not one shot did he get, and already the long hours had worn away half the night. Stillness covered the lake like a mantle, and brooded over it like a foreboding of evil, so that when at long intervals the far-off cry of a panther or the splash

of a fish on the water broke the quiet for an instant, the fleeting
noise seemed only to make the silence more oppressive. Suddenly he perceived the two fiery balls by the lake-side, though there
was no crackling of twigs ; the silence seemed deeper than ever,
but there were the bright eyes. For a moment he hesitated, then
pulled the bow-string, when out on the night air rung such a shriek
of wild inhuman pain that his arm fell at his side, and his heart
stopped with terror. No more shooting that night, so he hastily
guided his canoe across the lake, and climbed up the high side of
Overlook, to escape the dismal neighborhood of the lake. On the
top were dry leaves in plenty, and parched corn, all hidden in a
cave he knew of, and, making for that, he soon satisfied his hunger,
and prepared his bed for the few remaining hours before dawn.
Passing out to a little spring in the hill-side, he stooped beside a
great hollow log to quench his thirst. He suddenly felt himself
seized by the leg, and, reaching out, clutched a warm human hand.
Out from the log he dragged an Indian maiden, whose features he
could now see by the light of the rising moon to be convulsed
with terror. Her fears being soothed, she told him her story.

She said she had become separated from her tribe with her
sister, as they were on a hunting expedition on these mountains,
and they had wandered together through the trackless wilderness,
suffering untold agonies. This Overlook Mountain, she said, was
infested with vampires, who nightly pursued them to suck their
blood. Exhausted at last, they had sunk down and fallen asleep.
How long they slept she could not tell, but early in the night,
while Haidoni had been hunting on the lake, she was awakened
by a sound as of some one eating and drinking beside her.
Starting up, she beheld a vampire sucking her sister's blood and
eating her flesh, now dead. His form was so frightful, with its
long beard dripping blood and great glaring eyes of fire, that she

fled through the woods wildly seeking a hiding-place. The vampire, not relishing the loss of so dainty a meal, pursued her closely,
giving forth a fearful war-whoop! (Fancy a ghost with a war-

PILGRIM'S PASS.

whoop!) Sliding quickly into the hollow log, the vampire rushed
past her, not seeing, and probably passed on to the lake-side, for
not long after she heard a terrific shriek, and the echoes repeating
it by the shores of the hill-bound water.

"He is dead, then," said Haidoni, "for I shot, a short while since, a creature which was no deer, and its death yell was what you have heard."

TURTLE ROCK.

The young squaw went with her deliverer, and after several more meetings with vampires that night, and victories over the same, she concluded to remain with so valiant a warrior and go with him to his tribe. His arrows were thenceforth accounted to be invincible by reason of Manitou's favor, as no man else could kill so dread a demon as a vampire.

From Overlook to Plattekill Clove is perhaps the most beautiful drive the mountains afford. The trees have been cut away at intervals, giving glimpses of the valley below. The road runs all along the ridge of the mountain, and on that delicious September day, when the travellers, with whom our interest lies at present, passed over it, all the energies of nature seemed to have been put forth

BEFORE OLD MOUNT HOUSE.

to adorn it. A damp wood odor arose like incense, and the ground beneath the trees was a painted carpet of lush green moss sprinkled with gray-haired lichens, while the bloodroot and an occasional fallen leaf, turned gray, red, or yellow, made just the touches of color that the picture needed. The birches, those vestal virgins of the woods, stood, white and still, gleaming far within the cool forest depths, and the maples were donning their gay raiment, for October was not far away. When will the people who flock hither from cities learn that the high festival time up here is later, when all the gorges and mountain sides are one blaze of color? They see it from the river as they come down from a late sojourn at Lake George or Saratoga; they cry out in delighted surprise at the wonderful rose-purple in which the Catskills are bathed, but they pass on down, content without nearer inspection. Think how they

look when Indian summer has crept up the cloves and some wise old habitué goes following after to see the wonders that are there. The glory that covers them then might wellnigh turn one's head with a

STYLES GORGE AND PULPIT ROCK.   kind of delirium of beauty, and yet the great caravansaries of hotels are closed, the summer boarder has departed, and silence reigns in the rocky fastnesses.

On this day of which I write, some regret was expressed that travellers could not find bed and board here in the wonderful

season of turning leaves. Everybody said that "next year it must
be managed, really next year we must come in October."

POET'S BENCH, OVERLOOK.

Here let us take up Miss Rutherford's journal, an adjunct to
her travelling gear the which she cared for most religiously; "for,"
said she, "if I do not write it up each day I should get all these

waterfalls, and ravines, and devil's cauldrons, and kitchens,
and stairways so inextricably confused that five years hence I
should find myself describing Haines' Falls as running down Overlook Mountain, or that dreadful ' Black Chasm ' we went to on
our way to Plattekill Clove, as yawning under the old Mountain
House."

LOVER'S RETREAT, OVERLOOK.

Thursday, *Sept.
22d.*—Enjoyed a charm-
ing day in true moun-
taineer fashion, but
feel the effects of the
climbing and walking,
in a strained sensation
all over the body and
a strong desire to get
to bed. We begun the
day in fine spirits, for
this air invigorates like
wine, and one danger
of the place is said to be
this very effect of light-
ness and elasticity that
comes to you, for, under
its stimulating influence
many people overtax themselves, and pay the penalty when
again on *terra firma.* (There, I still preserve the delusion of walking on air, that has haunted me all day!)

We started immediately after breakfast on our tramp, leaving
groups of less enterprising pleasure seekers lounging about the
piazzas, or discoursing after the usual manner of tourists on the
cliff. How far you can see with and without a glass seems to

absorb the entire attention of most people, and a condition of
atmosphere in which the capitol at Albany (by a slight stretch of
imagination) can be seen from a cliff half a mile away, engenders
more excitement than a fine sunset or a mist-mantled moon.
This latter sight we were permitted to behold this evening.
Little breezes tore the mist into shreds and patches, and blew it
away in soft clouds from the face of Diana. It was a noiseless,
mysterious battle between the gods of the upper air, and the seat
of war seemed not fifty feet from our faces. She has conquered,

BOWLING.

has my lady Moon, for I could not have left the cliff with the battle
undecided, and now sails serenely over our heads, turning the few
clouds that still fly by beneath us into effulgent silver down, an
intangible substance belonging to some other world, whereon, for
aught I know, the old deities may once more ride or recline when
these watchful mortal eyes of ours are closed.

Mr. Grant said we must find a point below the ledge where a
wonderful view could be got, but he was n't sure whether it was

"Inspiration Rock" or "Turtle Rock," or a "devil's kitchen";
on second thoughts, he felt positive it was a poet's something.
Somebody asked if he was sure it was n't "Lovers' Retreat."
There did not seem to be any reason for Polly Perkins to blush.
If any thing could be wanting to complete the vulgarity of that sort
of remark, it is for some inconsequent woman to blush.

I should like to stay here a week, for these beautiful walks
need a more careful inspection, though I stored up enough loveli-

OVERLOOK PLAYGROUND.

ness in my mind to last a long time. We came home at noon
with great armfuls of maiden-hair fern, and harebells, and sweet
fern, and partridge vines, not to mention the birch-bark and queer
fungi and lichens. No doubt we shall throw them all away as too
burdensome before we reach New York. I am already filled with
regret at despoiling the woods of them.

After dinner we lounged awhile, and then watched a game of
billiards; this, with a short walk and an hour in the bowling-alley,
finished the day.

Of all the views, I suppose nothing here is so wonderful as
that from the tower, though some little feeling I had of dissatisfac-
tion with it seemed to be expressed in a remark of our Artist—" It
lacks foreground." You want a near object of comparison.

Foreground or not though, it inspires one with a sort of exalta-
tion, and quite justifies Mr. Grant's remark : " I should think a
race of artists ought to spring up here, if nature has any influence
over the spirit of man."

I found a prom-
ising instance of his
theory to-day in a
boy—a bare-legged,
big-hatted, indige-
nous boy—who was
drawing pictures with
a stone on the smooth
surface of a flat rock ;
but, alas ! for the in-
spiration of the
mighty hills, I found
on closer inspection

BOY ARTIST (GUIDE).

he was trying his " prentice hand " on a caricature of a distraught
looking youth from the hotel, whom he had set down as an
amateur poet !

Friday, *Sept. 23d.*—Enjoyed a delightful drive across the
mountains this morning, and down through Plattekill Clove, from
there to Saugerties, taking in Caatsban on the way. The Plattekill
is to my mind the finest clove of all, and nothing could be finer
than that one grand sweep—the Horse-Shoe Curve, they call it, I believe,—and the view from there is very fine out through the gorge,
showing a section of the valley—that is, if one has the heart to look,

BLACK CHASM.

which, I confess, I had not. With our wagon creaking and rocking on the very edge of a yawning chasm, I could do little else but shut my teeth and pray that the brakes would hold as we went lurching down the mountain.

Captain Oldbore said we must turn out of our way a little to pass through Caatsban with its old stone church and its historical associations. We were very glad to adopt this suggestion, for we had plenty of time before the evening boat for New York left the dock at Saugerties, and we were very loath to leave this lovely country. So we turned northward, still keeping toward the sides, and watching with regretful eyes the grand old mountains as their softened outlines receded behind us.

TERRACE FALL, PLATTEKILL.

Caatsban is well worth while seeing, with its old stone houses and the church of ancient Dutch build. The latter is not much to look at now since the ruthless people have "modernized" it, putting a white painted wooden steeple on it, but as it stands facing the road which climbs a gradually ascending hill, its position

THE HELL HOLE.

is very imposing, and nothing could be prettier than the picture one readily conjures up of the congregation, A. D. 1750, as they wended their way up this very road to morning service in quaint Holland costume.

Before you come to the church there is an old stone house, higher than ordinary, built a little way back from the road, with that quaint look at the gable end, of a woman with her hair parted in the middle and smoothed meekly down over her ears. The front yard is a grove of high poplars ; altogether the place has an old-world haunted look, and even its ghosts would seem foreign fancy. Think of all the ghosts talking Dutch, as they must, of course, in this region.

From Caatsban we struck down toward the river road to take in a great dreary

PLATTEKILL CLOVE.

marsh called "The Gröt Vly" or "Big Swamp." I do not know whether that is good Dutch or not ; it is the vernacular. John Grant gave us a story about it which I append here to my journal as a souvenir of this interesting place.

THE GRÖT VLY'S VICTIM.

HOOSING the low level ridges that skirt the foot of the Catskills, with a discernment unrivalled in the history of early Dutch highways, runs the "Old King's Road," as it has been called since it served the post-carriers in old colony days. The comparative directness of that road and its easy rises, you will never realize till you have been obliged to make a hurried journey across country by any of the ways laid out by the old settlers, and then you will find yourself obliged to wind over hills and through valleys in a way that produces very picturesque impressions of the scenery, but equally vivid convictions concerning the deserts of that Dutchman who made the journey ten miles long, when, as the bird flies, it was but four. However, nobody has any business to be in a hurry in this region, and, with human nature's true perversity, you resent in this case the very directness of the route that hurries you past such vistas of peaceful fields and winding streams.

Nothing could be lovelier than the views of the mountains toward the west, or of the Hudson River on the east, that open between trees or around jutting corners of the curious formation of rocks, whose perpendicular sides guard the way for a long distance like fortresses. Along this highway in the stirring times of the Revolution, passed many and strange figures—Whig and Tory, Indian and British spy, stout vrouws and blushing maidens, on errands of loyalty or treachery, love or hate, and each carried a weapon of defence, whether blunderbuss, pistol, or knife, hidden in the bosom. The whole way is rife with memories of old days, and the aroma of Indian superstition.

On a commanding hill stands Caatsban church, with a settlement of farm-houses clustered about it much as chickens huddle about the mother hen for protection. Over toward the river stretches away the black waste of marsh called by the Dutch the Gröt Vly, holding in its bottomless depths one of those Indian demons that the Dutch held in very respectful veneration, for heathen deities of fell power. This particular old deity seemed to have a special love for young girls, and more particularly for those who were already held in like estimation by the more attractive gallants of flesh and blood. Certain it is that on certain nights of the year he was wont to rise up from his watery bed, when woe to the luckless woman, beloved of man, who might be wandering near!

At the time of which I write, Burgoyne was advancing on Saratoga, the British were holding New York, and this broad river-valley was one of the most important keys to unlock the problem of the Revolution. The staunch Dutch were holding out well, keeping strict watch of Tory neighbors, lest some messenger should get up or down the valley to effect a junction of British forces, but rumors finally came that Brant was advancing toward the mountains from Niagara, and that thought brought dismay to even their stout hearts.

One September evening the mountains were hurling down shot and shell of a mightier kind than human hand could devise. The thunder and lightning came booming and flashing through the clove as if the great Manitou who dwells in their secret places had determined to vent his wrath on the dwellers below. In vain, however, did they besiege the parsonage where Domine Van Vlierden and his family sat around the great fire in peace and safety. The smoke from the good man's pipe ascended the blazing cavern on one side the hearth, while on the other side sat his broad wife, with placid, close-capped face, knitting stockings that might have been meant for a giant, so wide in the calf and long in the leg were they. The Domine was one of those pastors who played so important a part in the early history of New York State, and who were to the people of their respective parishes at once pastor, magistrate, physician, and military leader. He had a shrewd eye, and beneath his outer appearance of lethargy was a quick brain. With an education acquired at Leyden, and a manner and method of speech above his parishioners, he readily gained over them a great power, and ruled his people, from Catskill to Kingston and far beyond the mountains, with the undisputed sway of an autocrat, while his wife, styled by the country people the "Yvrouw," ruled him in turn. The two children crouching in the corner of the great settle were miniature copies, in face, figure, and dress, of their parents.

"It will be a great storm, Yvrouw," said the domine, using the vernacular then growing among the North River Dutch; "best get te kindern to bet."

As the wife rose to carry out this suggestion, a terrific blast shook the door on its great brass hinges, threatening to tear apart the two halves, and she paused as if listening to a knock. Just then another and fiercer blast drove in the upper door, bringing with it a hurricane of wind and rain, and displaying the figure of a woman thrown in strong relief against the outer blackness by the rays from the fire.

"Got in de himelin!" cried the now frightened Yvrouw, while the children shuddered and shrank still farther into their corner. The domine, however, went and pulled in the stranger and barred the door. Who was she? some spirit driven down the wild clove in the storm, or a spy? To the wife and children she seemed the former, but the domine's darkened brow gave out his suspicions of the latter. The slaves from the outer kitchen, having heard the clatter and bang, were now chattering and crowding in the inner door-way, their eyes wide with terror, while the children's fairly started from their heads, and they held up their arms before their faces as a defence.

Something absurd in the picture before her seemed to strike the new-comer, for glancing around her she lifted her head, letting fall the hood of her cloak, and laughed a long silvery peal, very unlike the usual "haw-haws" of the country side. This seemed to break the spell, for a torrent of questions was now poured forth, to all of which there was no answer save a smiling shake of the head and a reiterated inquiry for "Pierre Dubois." Now Pierre Dubois was a French Huguenot who lived a mile farther on the road, and nothing could be done that night but get the poor girl dry and then to bed, waiting for morning to bring Pierre, when he was expected to join the domine in a trip to the part of the parish that lay beyond the mountains. So the blacks were sent off to their quarters, the children hurried to bed, and then dry garments brought to replace the foreign looking clothes in which the stranger was clad. As she sat by the fire drying her wavy black locks, the domine eyed well her beautiful face with the soft eyes and the brilliant expression, thinking she was not at all like Pierre or Pierre's sort of folk. Pierre was short and stooping, while her figure was slim and tall with a sort of commanding carriage. As for the Yvrouw, she watched over the clicking needles, being rather distrustful of her strange appearing, illuminated so against the outer blackness; and then her very clothes were uncanny, the red-lined cloak and high-waisted, clinging skirts being any thing but Dutch in their pretty fashioning.

Morning brought light on the dark subject. The Yvrouw was awakened at early dawn by the same ringing laughter that startled her the previous night, and hurrying down stairs she found Pierre already arrived, and talking with the stranger in the open door-way. The man's face was a picture of horrified surprise; he stood stupidly staring, but the lady came forward and kissed the Yvrouw's hand saying, in her sweet voice, "*Bon jour, madame!*" Charmed, in spite of her stolid self, at the winning gesture, the Yvrouw looked inquiringly at Pierre, who seemed to have so scanty a welcome for this traveller. The girl spoke to him quickly in French, and this seemed to rouse his wandering wits.

"Oh, yes," he said hurriedly, "this will be my—my niece, your ladyship—I mean Yvrouw, who has come all the way from Paris to me here, and she was brought last night from Sopus in all the storm! Mon dieu, mon dieu!" he said, throwing up his hands, "to think that the winds and rains of heaven should dare to beat on that head!"

His wild gesture receiving a warning glance from the head in question, stopped all further speech on his part till soon the domine appeared on the scene. Then it was explained that his niece spoke only French, having, however, a little knowledge of the English, and she wished to teach embroidery and fine needle-work to the women and children as soon as she could learn enough of the language. Old Pierre begged that she might remain with the Yvrouw, as she was not used to the hardships and rough living of his family.

"She came from beautiful Paris, you know, sir, whilst I have lived most of my life in Provence."

So at last it was all arranged, and Sophie Dubois settled down into the ways of the parsonage, translating herself into a spirit of usefulness.

"It vill be vondershone vat Sophie ken do," said the Yvrouw very soon, "from the domine to te kindern, she vill pe for help-ing us." With her wit and high spirits she soon became the delight not only of the parsonage, but of the whole community, and no husking-bee or frolic was complete without her. She taught them pretty dances and strange foreign games; she sang songs grave and gay, till tears and laughter dwelt together on their honest faces, and yet she never came to be quite one of themselves. There were limits to her reserve which the boldest could not pass, and there breathed no gallant so bold that he had yet dared to offer her the customary salute when the red ear of corn came up at the husking, or when the sleighing parties jumped over a " kissing-hole " in the road. Her chief charm to these imaginative people lay in her gift of story-telling. She was a born *raconteur* to the tips of her facile fingers, and in the long winter evenings, as they gathered about some hospitable hearth, no prize was so coveted as Sophie in one of her happy moods. She was not all sunshine and fair weather though; sometimes she would say not a word for any one, only sit gazing in the fire with wide, sad eyes, and then they would whisper " She vill pe for getting homesick." She asked no sympathy and told nobody her thoughts at such times, but when the mood was right, how she poured forth her treasures of song and tale to their waiting ears!

No one of them all drank in her charms so eagerly as Garretje Brit, who sat always in a sort of silent worship in the chimney-corner, with knees curved, smoking his evening pipe. Every turn of her perfect head, each quick gesture, each flash of her smile, and tone of her voice when she sang or spoke, passed through his heart like an electric current. He followed her with little unobtrusive services, bringing her flowers and gorgeous October leaves, taking her, when she would suffer it, to church or to the country frolics. Nor was she unconscious of his devotion, but watched him now with amused interest as a mother might regard a diverting child, or again repulsed him almost fiercely if his hand chanced to touch her hair as he clumsily helped her with her cloak. Old Pierre saw all this with growing concern and sometimes spoke to her in her own language words that either caused her to laugh wickedly, or to answer with a haughty air more suggestive of the relation of master and servant than of niece and uncle.

One night there was a great husking over at the Bught (a " bight " or bend in the river near Catskill), and the young folks, with many of the older, of all the country side, from West Camp to the Van Bergen Patent, in great ark-like pungs, or on horseback, came riding down to enjoy the fun. There were the Abiels and the Snyders, the Wyncoops and Van Gelders, and the Heermans, the Kiersteds, and the Van Ordens, with a sprinkling of Scotch, as seasoning for the polyglot pie, in the persons of the Salisburys and Grants from Leeds-way, while the Huguenot element was represented by the Leferves, the Frères, and the Eltinges. Then there were some Germans from the Palatinate, settled across the river, such as the Allendorphs, the Stickles, and the Hommels. The babel produced by these different nationalities baffles description, for the language of the region had developed into a vernacular in which remained words of each tongue, but the whole sounded like broken English. The jaw-breaking words flew back and forth like the fast flying ears of corn. The huge raftered barn, the mows piled up with hay, the horses poking their sniffing noses through their stall windows, candles stuck here and there, and the groups of jolly Dutch in their quilted petticoats, or knee-breeches and long worsted stockings, all combined to make a picture worthy the brush of some old Holland master. By and by comes the hostess surging along like a great scow among smaller craft, bumping against this one and that one, saying : " Now den once for de victuals,—come eat till you burst, and I wish you may ! " Indeed it would seem that the company would need to accomplish some such gastronomic feat if the supper were to be disposed of that night. Great wooden dishes and troughs were piled high with two whole sheep, an entire bear, and smaller piles of chickens, turkeys, sausage, crullers, volichie, apple-butter, and other dainties, all set forth cheek by jowl, and served to each guest on one large dish. One chronicler asserts that often as many as a hundred chickens and an equal number of turkeys and ducks were devoured at these feasts. Sophie Dubois looked on with amused disgust while the supper went on, refusing all refreshment but a glass of cider, thereby bringing down on herself the distressed importunities of the hostess and her final indignant despair. After the feast came the dancing, and a meal such as would have incapacitated an ordinary mortal from stirring from his chair, seemed to animate their usually spiritless bodies with an unwonted vivacity. As the fun grew more furious, a luckless wight was emboldened to steal a sly kiss from Sophie where she stood in the shadow regarding the antics on the barn floor. Encircling her waist with his arm he reached toward her shrinking face, regardless of her struggles, when a sound "thwack!" laid him sprawling on the floor, where Garretje Brit stood over him saying: "Take dat, te gret awkward Onwijzen!" A great laugh greeted this confusion, and Sophie stole a grateful look at Garretje that caused his heart to bound. Afterward he saw her shiver and heard her mutter between her closed teeth: "The impertinent! The dog!" He could not help rejoicing that the lady of his love was unlike these girls with their indiscriminate favors, and yet why should the peasant niece of Pierre Dubois be so proud? And what made old Pierre himself look just now as if he had seen some impious thing done, as if the brass-bound Bible itself had been hurled from the pulpit? After all, one should not give one's self airs.

So the winter wore away in work and occasional pleasuring, and in the spring with the blossoms and birds, and the warm south winds came also rumors of trouble in the air. Brant was surely on his way from Niagara with a great band of Indians, and two or three English officers. The men of the region were enlisted in the army of the rebellion, as the British called it, but Garretje Brit had been one of a little company who stayed at home, scenting afar off the danger that was to come upon these unprotected firesides in the method of attack the mother country afterward adopted, when she set a price on Whig scalps and sent the red men to harry the homes left unguarded under the mountains.

As the summer passed, Sophie's face grew thinner and paler, and she seemed at times possessed by a feverish expectation of some event that was to come. At such times the color would come back to her cheeks, and her step regain its spring as she wandered restlessly through the meadows. Garretje warned her against these lonely wanderings in vain, she only smiled and paid no heed, so he took to following her at a distance or meeting her at any unexpected turn in the path. Then she would wake up like any sleep-walker, sometimes seeming annoyed at the intrusion on her dreams, at others so kind and sweet that the poor fellow would be in rapture. Once while she stood watching the current of the creek where it winds through the " Vlaats," or flat-lands, Garretje came upon her suddenly, and she looked so sad and dejected with her hands clasped behind her and head bent down, a very picture of despair in the warm sunset light, that his heart was flooded with a sense of her loveliness and loneliness. Something of his feeling burst from him almost unaware. She looked up as if puzzled to make out his meaning, and then seemed interested. Finally her eyes softened and filled with tears, and she put out her hand to stop him.

" Oh, no, dear Garretje ! I am not what you think—it could not be—oh, never, never ! "

He was kneeling now at her feet, sobbing like a child, and she put her hand pityingly on his head. It was a pretty, pathetic picture, but to Pierre Dubois going along with a bundle of rushes on his shoulders it seemed to present some other element, for he stood still a little way off, trembling and scared. Sophie spying him as he stood there laughed aloud at his absurd plight. Poor Garretje started up as if stung, and Sophie cried with a touch of bitterness : " *Ah, mon bon Pierre, comme les dieus sont tombés !* " The next moment she was hurrying after her would-be lover, calling in her sweetest accents : " Please, oh please forgive me ! "

Old Pierre collected his wits and resumed his journey, muttering to himself : " We are all but dogs in her proud eyes, and yet I would serve her mother's child to my death! "

One autumn night when the leaves had turned their brightest tints, and the air had a frosty bite in its touch, some neighbors had gathered about the domine's hearth to listen to Sophie's songs and tales. A wealth of warmth and light poured from the vast chimney to meet the path of the moonbeams on the polished floor, playing strange freaks on its way with the stolid faces it touched as it passed. The young girl was in a strangely excited mood, and her eyes shone like stars, while her stories were all of love and war and danger.

At the conclusion of one that was all about " a warrior bold with spurs of gold," who had rescued his lady from her enemies, and died at last in her service, she exclaimed : " So it was they loved in old Provence a hundred years ago ! Never then did a knight break faith or forget—oh, no !—and it was reward enough to die for love ! "

" It vass petter to die in te service of Got," said Garretje, solemnly; "end, pesides, there pe no maids any more who can lofe much."

She turned her eyes from the fire with an impatient little frown, as if a child had interrupted.

"It was the nobles, Garretje. You comprehend it not—how could you? But, piff!" with a scornful wave of her hands, as she unclasped them from her knees where she sat on the low stool, "'t is no more so. I dare swear there was this many a year in all fair France but one maiden who would cross an ocean to meet a lover, and he—perhaps," with a break in her voice.—" he would fail her!"

Then she drew back in the shadow and leaned her head against the chimney jamb, looking sadly toward the window, where the Virginia creeper outside fluttered back and forth in the breeze, tracing graceful arabesques on the tiny moonlit panes. Garretje, repulsed, put in his proper place, gazed on her longingly across the path of the fire-light, and it seemed to him an impassable gulf, with her face far off and faint on the other side, and her eyes looking ever away into another world than his. Would she hear him if he called to her?

Old Pierre, too, was watching her covertly, and saw her start as if she saw more than the vine on the pane, and when she soon after slipped quietly out of the room, he stole after her, but she was nowhere to be seen. He took up his position by the hall door and waited patiently till she came back into the hall-way, with flushed cheeks and glad eyes.

"You look as if you had seen into heaven," he said, eying her narrowly; "and who was the man I saw out there?"

"*Peut-être,*" shrugging her shoulders, "it may be that I have just caught a glimpse through the blessed gates; but, old Pierre, you are fast losing your sight. As for the man, you saw your shadow!"

" My shadow wears no red coat, mademoiselle."

" *Ciel*, how you are stupid ! " bending low to look into his old face with mocking eyes. " May not I wear my coat *renversé*— wrong-side-out, if so it pleases me ! "

So she slipped back to her low seat beside the Yvrouw's knee, just as Tobias Terwilliger was finishing a legend of the Gröt Vly (Great Swamp) that stretches away behind the hill toward the river.

" Efen yet," said the old Boerman, " it is one moon of te year, end dis vill pe te moon, ven if any maid belofed py a youth valks by its edge, a gret arm rises outen te Vly end teks her down, but it must be at twelf of de clock at night ! "

An awe-struck silence here ensued, broken only by the puffs of the pipes, the click of knitting needles, and the sonorous breathing of one old man who had gone to sleep.

" Do you all believe that ?   Do you Garretje Brit ? "

It was Sophie Dubois who spoke, and many eyes turned toward her, remembering for many a long year how she looked that night.   There was about the girl an indefinable charm or fascination, something that drew all hearts and yet was independent of her beauty—something that comes not " by favor of blue eyes, or black, or brown," and yet her face was so lovely to-night that to these people its wonderful illuminated expression was wellnigh supernatural.   On the hand she held up, palm outward, to guard her cheek from the blaze, there glowed a ruby heart.

" You believe that, Garretje, I ask ? "   And he was fain to reply : " I shall not scorn to beleef what my fathers held to be truth."

Tall and slim she rose up in the fire-light, standing for a moment as if in thought, with her hands clasped loosely in front of her, then as if she had reached some inward decision, she bent over the good Yvrouw and kissed her three times. Rising, she looked around on the group, and with a wave of her hand said, as a queen might have addressed her subjects : " Good people— good-night ! " As she passed out behind Garretje, a soft touch on his shoulder and the odor of a jasmine flower falling in his lap, made his head swim and his heart stand still under the sweet electric influence of her presence, then she was gone. " Adieu, my good and dear Garretje ! " Was it only a fancy, or did she whisper that in his ear ?

Next morning, as he went over the hills at early dawn, toward the Bught, he still thought he heard the voice in his ears, but now it seemed to come from the Grot Vly, calling softly, " Adieu, O my Garretje, adieu ! " Drawn almost irresistibly toward the swamp, he walked aimlessly along the shores where the morning vapors came pouring off in a rose-tinted cloud. Wrapped in his dream, he saw and heard naught but the face and the voice of the previous night, though all the woods were waking up to life, and flapping crows were calling hoarsely through the fog, while the whole world was turning to rose and gold. Now his feet were tripping in some soft thing like a garment, and stooping, he picked up a woman's cloak lined with red. A cry went echoing through the woods that startled all the birds and sent the crows screaming back over the Vly, while Garretje fell prone upon the ground, in his great loss and sorrow.

The news of Sophie Dubois' awful fate, drawn into the Gröt Vly by the Indian demon, spread throughout the country, bringing sorrow to all, but old Pierre and his indifference were so shameful that the domine himself was drawn to remonstrate. No word did he answer, however, to the charge, but this : " Domine, 't is no time for bewailing ; dey say Brant is on South Mountain, and a British spy escaped last night, going right through our midst to de river, to join de ship *Vulture* de British have brought to anchor down by Sopus ! "

" Got in de himelen ! " cried the domine, " mount a horse den, end rouse de country, vile I puckle on my sword end get dat militia to de church ! "

So the old church was turned into barracks and such drilling of raw recruits, such cleaning of old weapons, and such gun practice, was never witnessed before or since.

During the years that followed till peace was declared, and the British evacuated New York, so much of hardship and sorrow came to these people of Caatsban, that poor Sophie's fate was seldom spoken of, but at last in the quiet time succeeding peace, there came to the Yvrouw a letter with a great armorial seal half covering one side. It was signed " Sophie Montmorenci-Sackville," and it thanked the good Yvrouw, in many graceful and fervent phrases, for her great kindness to the writer, who had fled from her home in France and from her father, the Marquis de Montmorenci, to join her lover in America. The lover who was forbidden her was an officer in the English army, hence an enemy to her family. Colonel Sackville had come from Canada under the guidance of Brant, and had joined her, as previously arranged between them, at Caatsban, fleeing thence with her to the ship *Vulture* down the river, where they were married. She had purposely deceived them as to her fate, the better to protect her husband in his dangerous flight. She wished to be kindly remembered to old Pierre Dubois who had " helped me in grateful memory of my mother, on whose family estates in Provence he had formerly lived as a dependent ; likewise to Garretje Brit, whose friendship I shall ever cherish as a valued possession." With the letter came also a chest filled with presents from Colonel Sackville to " my wife's kind friends and protectors," among which was a store

of finery for the good Yvrouw Van Vlierden, much too grand for
her simple tastes and frugal life.   The gowns and laces were laid
away in lavender and linen, and handed down to her descendants.
They came finally into the possession of the Myer family of Saugerties, where in '82 they were destroyed in a burning farm-house.

As for Garretje Brit he would accept none of the fine presents,
but when he died years after, a lonely old man, they found about
his neck a little locket hanging from a cord, and when they opened
it, there was only a shrivelled flower exhaling a faint odor of jasmine.

Passing through Saugerties we saw some more fine old Dutch
houses, and were surprised to find the town so large and flourishing ; some of the streets were very pretty with their high-arching
shade trees and smooth lawns, all kept carefully fenced, however.
I was curious to see more of the town, said to be so proud of its
Dutch ancestry, and was much interested in the names, scores of
them with a jaw-breaking Dutch sound, and the old spelling preserved intact.   As for the name of the town itself, all the information I procured seemed to indicate its Dutch extraction.   The
tract on which the town was built belonged to a sawyer, "sager,"
who on account of his small size was called "sager-tje," the affix
"tje" being a diminutive often found in their names, the possessive

added to this word then made it " sagertje's," the property of the little sawyer.

I don't know why, but somehow the personality of that little sawyer has grown to be of intense interest to me, and indeed I went out to the little creek called " Sagers-kill," or as they have it now " Sau-kill," where his old mill stood, and where now a grist mill grinds its daily task.

I fancied that he came out on the bridge (there must surely have been a bridge then, before this modern iron thing was thought of), and smoked his pipe to the rosy sunsets, while his eyes wandered far over the valley toward the mountains all aglow with the evening light. No doubt his thoughts were more of work and gain than of the transfiguration that had come to those distant hills, but I like to think his slow Dutch mind was penetrated with some of the wonder of the picture.

There was much to admire in those ancestors of ours, and much to be proud of and grateful for. Such abiding strength was ingrained in their distinctive traits that they seem to have been impressed on the faces of the race to this day, so that in these places where the Holland blood predominates you can now and then read in the passing countenances the old pluck, the bravery that resisted to the death, the unswerving honesty, and, most prominent of all, the even-tempered but unyielding and mulish obstinacy.

*　　　*　　　*　　　*　　　*　　　*

Alas, that I must write that ugly little word *finis* to this most perfect of pilgrimages !

We watched from the deck of the night boat the last lingering rays of sunset behind those enchanted hills, and then turned doleful faces to each other to be commiserated on the close of our holiday. I heard Polly say in her breathless, excited way to Mr.

John Grant : " Oh, if I could have but one wish granted in all this world, I should wish for one of those mountains to be transported to some spot where I could always see the sun set behind it from my window!"

" I know what I should wish for, if I had but one wish," answered her companion.

" What would that be ? "

The answer to this leading question was too low for my ears to catch, but I suspect that two young people in our party found something in that magical region of the Catskills that is to them, at least, as rare, and far more precious than Manitou's treasure.

We consoled ourselves later in the evening by listening to Mr. Grant's reading of that prettiest of all American tales, so familiar to us all, Irving's " Rip Van Winkle." As it formed the prologue to our summer idyl, acting as the inspiration from which our journey sprung, it shall be its epilogue, and never again can I doubt its truth, for have I not been there ; have I not sat in Rip's chair, and seen the print of his gun on the rock !

THE LEGEND OF RIP VAN WINKLE.

A Posthumous Writing of Diedrich Knickerbocker, From Irving's "Sketch-Book."

By Woden, God of Saxons,
From whence comes Wensday, that is Wodensday,
Truth is a thing that ever I will keep,
Unto thylke day in which I creep into
My sepulchre—   *Cartwright.*

Whoever has made a voyage up the Hudson must remember the Kaatskill Mountains. They are a dismembered branch of the great Appalachian family, and are seen away to the west of the river, swelling up to a noble height, and lording it over the surrounding country. Every change of season, every change of weather, indeed, every hour of the day, produces some change in the magic hues and shapes of these mountains; and they are regarded by all the good wives, far and near, as perfect barometers. When the weather is fair and settled, they are clothed in blue and purple, and print their bold outlines on the clear evening sky ; but sometimes, when the rest of the landscape is cloudless, they will gather a hood of gray vapors about their summits, which, in the last rays of the setting sun, will glow and light up like a crown of glory.

At the foot of these fairy mountains the voyager may have descried the light smoke curling up from a village, whose shingle roofs gleam among the trees just where the blue tints of the up-

land melt away into the fresh green of the nearer landscape. It is
a little village of great antiquity, having been founded by some of
the Dutch colonists in the early times of the province, just about
the beginning of the government of the good Peter Stuyvesant
(may he rest in peace!) ; and there were some of the houses of the
original settlers standing within a few years, built of small yellow
bricks brought from Holland, having latticed windows and gable
fronts, surmounted with weathercocks.

In that same village, and in one of these very houses (which,
to tell the precise truth, was sadly time-worn and weather-beaten),
there lived many years since, while the country was yet a province
of Great Britain, a simple, good-natured fellow, of the name of Rip
Van Winkle. He was a descendant of the Van Winkles who fig-
ured so gallantly in the chivalrous days of Peter Stuyvesant, and
accompanied him to the siege of Christina. He inherited, however, but little of the martial character of his ancestors. I have
observed that he was a simple, good-natured man ; he was, moreover, a kind neighbor, and an obedient, henpecked husband. Indeed, to the latter circumstance might be owing that meekness of
spirit which gained him such universal popularity ; for those men
are most apt to be obsequious and conciliating abroad who are
under the discipline of shrews at home. Their tempers, doubtless,
are rendered pliant and malleable in the fiery furnace of domestic
tribulation ; and a curtain lecture is worth all the sermons in the
world for teaching the virtues of patience and long-suffering. A
termagant wife may, therefore, in some respects, be considered a
tolerable blessing ; and, if so, Rip Van Winkle was thrice blessed.

Certain it is that he was a great favorite among all the good
wives of the village, who, as usual with the amiable sex, took his
part in all family squabbles, and never failed, whenever they talked
those matters over in their evening gossipings, to lay all the blame

on Dame Van Winkle. The children of the village, too, would
shout with joy whenever he approached. He assisted at their sports,
made their playthings, taught them to fly kites and shoot marbles,
and told them long stories of ghosts, witches, and Indians. Whenever he went dodging about the village, he was surrounded by a
troop of them, hanging on his skirts, clambering on his back, and
playing a thousand tricks on him with impunity ; and not a dog
would bark at him throughout the neighborhood.

The great error in Rip's composition was an insuperable aversion to all kinds of profitable labor. It could not be from want of
assiduity or perseverance ; for he would sit on a wet rock with a
rod as long and heavy as a Tartar's lance, and fish all day without
a murmur, even though he should not be encouraged by a single
nibble. He would carry a fowling-piece on his shoulder for hours
together, trudging through woods and swamps, and up hill and
down dale, to shoot a few squirrels or wild pigeons. He would
never refuse to assist a neighbor, even in the roughest toil, and
was a foremost man at all country frolics for husking Indian corn
or building stone fences. The women of the village, too, used to
employ him to run their errands, and to do such little odd jobs as
their less obliging husbands would not do for them,—in a word,
Rip was ready to attend to anybody's business but his own ; but
as to doing family duty, and keeping his farm in order, he found it
impossible.

In fact he declared it was of no use to work on his farm ; it
was the most pestilent little piece of ground in the whole country ;
every thing about it went wrong and would go wrong in spite of
him. His fences were continually falling to pieces ; his cows
would either go astray or get among the cabbages ; weeds were
sure to grow quicker in his fields than anywhere else ; the rain
always made a point of setting in just as he had some out-door

work to do; so that his patrimonial estate had dwindled away under his management, acre by acre, until there was little more left than a mere patch of Indian corn and potatoes, yet it was the worst-conditioned farm in the neighborhood.

His children, too, were as ragged and wild as if they belonged to nobody. His son Rip, an urchin begotten in his own likeness, promised to inherit the habits with the old clothes of his father. He was generally seen trooping like a colt at his mother's heels, equipped in a pair of his father's cast-off galligaskins, which he had much ado to hold up with one hand, as a fine lady does her train in bad weather.

Rip Van Winkle, however, was one of those happy mortals, of foolish, well-oiled dispositions, who take the world easy, eat white bread or brown, whichever can be got with least thought or trouble, and would rather starve on a penny than work for a pound. If left to himself, he would have whistled life away in perfect contentment; but his wife kept continually dinning in his ears about his idleness, his carelessness, and the ruin he was bringing on his family.

Morning, noon, and night, her tongue was incessantly going; and every thing he said or did was sure to produce a torrent of household eloquence. Rip had but one way of replying to all lectures of the kind; and that, by frequent use, had grown into a habit. He shrugged his shoulders, shook his head, cast up his eyes, but said nothing. This, however, always provoked a fresh volley from his wife, so that he was fain to draw off his forces, and take to the outside of the house, the only side which, in truth, belongs to a henpecked husband.

Rip's sole domestic adherent was his dog Wolf, who was as much henpecked as his master; for Dame Van Winkle regarded them as companions in idleness, and even looked upon Wolf with

an evil eye, as the cause of his master's going so often astray.
True it is, in all points of spirit befitting an honorable dog, he was
as courageous an animal as ever scoured the woods ; but what
courage can withstand the everduring and all-besetting terrors of
a woman's tongue? The moment Wolf entered the house his
crest fell, his tail dropped to the ground or curled between his
legs, he sneaked about with a gallows air, casting many a sidelong
glance at Dame Van Winkle, and at the least flourish of a broom-
stick or ladle he would fly to the door with yelping precipitation.

Times grew worse and worse with Rip Van Winkle as years
of matrimony rolled on ; a tart temper never mellows with age,
and a sharp tongue is the only edged tool that grows keener with
constant use. For a long while he used to console himself, when
driven from home, by frequenting a kind of perpetual club of the
sages, philosophers, and other idle personages of the village, which
held its sessions on a bench before a small inn, designated by a
rubicund portrait of His Majesty George III. Here they used to
sit in the shade, of a long lazy summer's day, talking listlessly over
village gossip, or telling endless sleepy stories about nothing. But
it would have been worth any statesman's money to have heard
the profound discussions which sometimes took place, when by
chance an old newspaper fell into their hands from some passing
traveller. How solemnly they would listen to the contents, as
drawled by Derrick Van Bummell, the school-master, a dapper,
learned little man, who was not to be daunted by the most gigantic word in the dictionary ; and how sagely they would deliberate
upon public events some months after they had taken place !

The opinions of this junto were completely controlled by
Nicholas Vedder, a patriarch of the village, and landlord of the
inn, at the door of which he took his seat from morning till night,
just moving sufficiently to avoid the sun, and keep in the shade of

a large tree ; so that the neighbors could tell the hour by his movements as accurately as by a sun-dial. It is true, he was rarely heard to speak, but smoked his pipe incessantly. His adherents, however (for every great man has his adherents), perfectly understood him, and knew how to gather his opinions. When any thing that was read or related displeased him, he was observed to smoke his pipe vehemently, and to send forth short, frequent, and angry puffs ; but when pleased, he would inhale the smoke slowly and tranquilly, and emit it in light placid clouds, and sometimes taking the pipe from his mouth, and letting the fragrant vapor curl about his nose, would gravely nod his head in token of perfect approbation.

From even this stronghold the unlucky Rip was at length routed by his termagant wife, who would suddenly break in upon the tranquillity of the assemblage, and call the members all to nought ; nor was that august personage, Nicholas Vedder himself, sacred from the daring tongue of this terrible virago, who charged him outright with encouraging her husband in habits of idleness.

Poor Rip was at last reduced almost to despair ; and his only alternative to escape from the labor of the farm and the clamor of his wife was to take gun in hand, and stroll away into the woods. Here he would sometimes seat himself at the foot of a tree, and share the contents of his wallet with Wolf, with whom he sympathized as a fellow-sufferer in persecution. " Poor Wolf ! " he would say, " thy mistress leads thee a dog's life of it ; but never mind, whilst I live thou shalt never want a friend to stand by thee." Wolf would wag his tail, look wistfully in his master's face ; and, if dogs can feel pity, I verily believe he reciprocated the sentiment with all his heart.

In a long ramble of the kind, on a fine autumnal day, Rip had unconsciously scrambled to one of the highest parts of the Kaats-

kill Mountains. He was after his favorite sport of squirrel-shoot-
ing, and the still solitudes had echoed and re-echoed with the
reports of his gun.   Panting and fatigued, he threw himself, late in
the afternoon, on a green knoll covered with mountain herbage,
that crowned the brow of a precipice.   From an opening between
the trees he could overlook all the lower country for many a mile
of rich woodland.   He saw at a distance the lordly Hudson, far, far
below him, moving on its silent but majestic course, with the
reflection of a purple cloud, or the sail of a lagging bark here and
there sleeping on its glassy bosom, and at last losing itself in
the blue highland.

On the other side he looked down into a deep mountain glen,
wild, lonely, and shagged, the bottom filled with fragments from
the impending cliffs, and scarcely lighted by the reflecting rays of
the setting sun.*   For some time Rip lay musing on this scene ;
evening was gradually advancing ; the mountains began to throw
their long blue shadows over the valleys ; he saw that it would
be dark long before he could reach the village ; and he heaved a
heavy sigh when he thought of encountering the terrors of Dame
Van Winkle.

As he was about to descend he heard a voice from a distance
hallooing, " Rip Van Winkle ! Rip Van Winkle ! " He looked
around, but could see nothing but a crow winging its solitary
flight across the mountain.   He thought his fancy must have
deceived him, and turned again to descend, when he heard the
same cry ring through the still evening air, " Rip Van Winkle !
Rip Van Winkle ! "—at the same time Wolf bristled up his back,
and, giving a low growl, skulked to his master's side, looking fear-
fully down into the glen.   Rip now felt a vague apprehension
stealing over him : he looked anxiously in the same direction, and

---

* The glen here described is passed by the visitor to the Mountain House during the first
mile of ascent in climbing the mountain.   It begins near the gate, and ends at the " Shanty."

perceived a strange figure slowly toiling up the rocks, and bending under the weight of something he carried on his back. He was surprised to see any human being in this lonely and unfrequented place; but, supposing it to be some one of the neighborhood in need of assistance, he hastened down to yield it.

On nearer approach, he was still more surprised at the singularity of the stranger's appearance. He was a short, square-built old fellow, with thick, brushy hair and a grizzled beard. His dress was of the antique Dutch fashion: a cloth jerkin strapped round the waist; several pairs of breeches, the outer one of ample volume, decorated with rows of buttons down the sides, and bunches at the knees. He bore on his shoulders a stout keg, that seemed full of liquor, and made signs for Rip to approach, and assist him with the load. Though rather shy and distrustful of this new acquaintance, Rip complied with his usual alacrity; and, mutually relieving each other, they clambered up a narrow gully, apparently the dry bed of a mountain torrent. As they ascended, Rip every now and then heard long, rolling peals, like distant thunder, that seemed to issue out of a deep ravine, or rather cleft between lofty rocks, toward which their rugged path conducted. He paused for an instant; but, supposing it to be the muttering of one of those transient thunder-showers which often take place in mountain heights, he proceeded. Passing through the ravine, they came to a hollow, like a small amphitheatre, surrounded by perpendicular precipices, over the banks of which impending trees shot their branches, so that you only caught glimpses of the azure sky and the bright evening cloud. During the whole time, Rip and his companion had labored on in silence; for though the former marvelled greatly what could be the object of carrying a keg of liquor up this wild mountain, yet there was something strange and incomprehensible about the unknown that inspired awe and checked familiarity.

On entering the amphitheatre, new objects of wonder presented themselves. On a level spot in the centre was a company of odd-looking personages playing at ninepins. They were dressed in a quaint, outlandish fashion : some wore short doublets, others jerkins, with long knives in their belts ; and most of them had enormous breeches, of similar style with that of the guide's. Their visages, too, were peculiar ; one had a large head, broad face, and small piggish eyes ; the face of another seemed to consist entirely of nose, and was surmounted by a white sugar-loaf hat, set off with a little red cock's tail. They all had beards, of various shapes and colors. There was one who seemed to be the commander. He was a stout old gentleman, with a weather-beaten countenance ; he wore a laced doublet, broad belt and hanger, high-crowned hat and feather, red stockings, and high-heeled shoes with roses in them. The whole group reminded Rip of the figures in an old Flemish painting, in the parlor of Dominie Van Shaick, the village parson, and which had been brought over from Holland at the time of the settlement.

What seemed particularly odd to Rip was, that though these folks were evidently amusing themselves, yet they maintained the gravest faces, the most mysterious silence, and were withal the most melancholy party of pleasure he had ever witnessed. Nothing interrupted the stillness of the scene but the noise of the balls, which, whenever they were rolled, echoed along the mountains like rumbling peals of thunder.

As Rip and his companion approached them they suddenly desisted from their play, and stared at him with such a fixed, statue-like gaze, and such strange, uncouth, lack-lustre countenances, that his heart turned within him, and his knees smote together. His companion now emptied the contents of the keg into large flagons, and made signs to him to wait upon the company. He obeyed with fear and trembling; they quaffed the liquor in profound silence, and then returned to their game.

By degrees Rip's awe and apprehension subsided. He even ventured, when no eye was fixed upon him, to taste the beverage, which he found had much of the flavor of excellent Hollands. He was naturally a thirsty soul, and was soon tempted to repeat the draught. One taste provoked another, and he reiterated his visits to the flagon so often, that at length his senses were overpowered, his eyes swam in his head, his head gradually declined, and he fell into a deep sleep.

On waking he found himself on the green knoll whence he had first seen the old man of the glen. He rubbed his eyes,— it was a bright sunny morning. The birds were hopping and twitting among the bushes, and the eagle was wheeling aloft and breasting the pure mountain breeze. "Surely," thought Rip, " I have not slept here all night." He recalled the occurrences before he fell asleep,—the strange man with the keg of liquor, the mountain ravine, the wild retreat among the rocks, the woe-begone party at ninepins, the flagon. " Oh! that wicked flagon!" thought Rip ; " what excuse shall I make to Dame Van Winkle ? "

He looked round for his gun ; but in place of the clean, well-oiled fowling-piece, he found an old firelock lying beside him, the barrel encrusted with rust, the lock falling off, and the stock worm-eaten. He now suspected that the grave roisters of the mountain had put a trick upon him, and, having dosed him with liquor, had robbed him of his gun. Wolf, too, had disappeared, but he might have strayed away after a squirrel or partridge. He whistled after him, and shouted his name, but all in vain ; the echoes repeated his whistle and shout, but no dog was to be seen.

He determined to revisit the scene of the last evening's gambol, and, if he met with any of the party, to demand his dog and gun. As he rose to walk, he found himself stiff in the joints, and wanting in his usual activity. " These mountain beds do not agree with me," thought Rip ; " and, if this frolic should lay me up with a fit of the rheumatism, I shall have a blessed time with Dame Van Winkle." With some difficulty he got down into the glen ; he found the gully up which he and his companion had ascended the preceding evening ; but to his astonishment a mountain stream was now foaming down it, leaping from rock to rock, and filling the glen with babbling murmurs. He, however, made shift to scramble up its sides, working his toilsome way through thickets of birch, sassafras, and witch-hazel, and sometimes tripped up or entangled by the wild grape-vines that twisted their coils and tendrils from tree to tree, and spread a kind of network in his path.

At length he reached to where the ravine had opened through the cliffs to the amphitheatre ; but no traces of such opening remained. The rocks presented a high, impenetrable wall, over which the torrent came tumbling in a sheet of feathery foam, and fell into a broad, deep basin, black from the shadows of the surrounding forest. Here, then, poor Rip was brought to a stand. He again called and whistled for his dog ; he was only answered by the cawing of a flock of idle crows, sporting high in air about a dry tree that overhung a sunny precipice, and who, secure in their elevation, seemed to look down and scoff at the poor man's perplexities. What was to be done ? The morning was passing away, and Rip felt famished for want of his breakfast. He grieved to give up his dog and gun ; he dreaded to meet his wife ; but it would not do to starve among the mountains. He shook his head, shouldered the rusty firelock, and, with a heart full of trouble and anxiety, turned his steps homeward.

As he approached the village he met a number of people, but none whom he knew, which somewhat surprised him, for he had thought himself acquainted with every one in the country round. Their dress, too, was of a different fashion from that to which he was accustomed. They all stared at him with equal marks of surprise, and whenever they cast eyes upon him, invariably stroked their chins. The constant recurrence of this gesture induced Rip involuntarily to do the same, when, to his astonishment, he found his beard had grown a foot long !

He had now entered the skirts of the village. A troop of strange children ran at his heels, hooting after him, and pointing at his gray beard. The dogs, too, not one of which he recognized for an old acquaintance, barked at him as he passed. The very village was altered ; it was larger and more populous. There were rows of houses which he had never seen before, and those which had been his familiar haunts had disappeared. Strange names were over the doors, strange faces at the windows ; every thing was strange. His mind now misgave him ; he began to doubt whether both he and the world around him were not bewitched. Surely this was his native village, which he had left but a day before. There stood the Kaatskill Mountains ; there ran the silver Hudson at a distance ; there was every hill and dale precisely as it had always been. Rip was sorely perplexed. " That flagon last night," thought he, " has addled my poor head sadly."

It was with some difficulty that he found the way to his house, which he approached with silent awe, expecting every moment to hear the shrill voice of Dame Van Winkle. He found the house gone to decay—the roof fallen in, the windows shattered, and the doors off the hinges. A half-starved dog, that looked like Wolf, was skulking about it. Rip called him by name ; but the cur snarled, showed his teeth, and passed on. This was an unkind cut indeed. "My very dog," sighed poor Rip, "has forgotten me."

He entered the house, which, to tell the truth, Dame Van Winkle had always kept in neat order. It was empty, forlorn, and apparently abandoned. This desolateness overcame all his connubial fears ; he called loudly for his wife and children ; the lonely chambers rang for a moment with his voice, and then all again was silence.

He now hurried forth, and hastened to his old resort, the village inn ; but it too was gone. A large, rickety wooden building stood in its place, with great gaping windows, some of them broken, and mended with old hats and petticoats, and over the door was painted, "The Union Hotel, by Jonathan Doolittle." Instead of the tree that used to shelter the quiet little Dutch inn of yore, there now was reared a tall, naked pole, with something on the top that looked like a red nightcap, and from it was fluttering a flag, on which was a singular assemblage of stars and stripes ; all this was strange and incomprehensible. He recognized on the sign, however, the ruby face of King George, under which he had smoked so many a peaceful pipe ; but even this was singularly metamorphosed. The red coat was changed for one of blue and buff ; a sword was held in the hand instead of a sceptre ; the head was decorated with a cocked hat ; and underneath was painted, in large characters, GENERAL WASHINGTON.

There was, as usual, a crowd of folk about the door, but none that Rip recollected. The very character of the people seemed changed. There was a busy, bustling, disputatious tone about it, instead of the accustomed phlegm and drowsy tranquillity. He looked in vain for the sage Nicholas Vedder, with his broad face, double chin, and fair long pipe, uttering clouds of tobacco-smoke instead of idle speeches ; or Van Bummel, the school-master, doling forth the contents of an ancient newspaper. In place of these, a lean, bilious-looking fellow, with his pockets full of handbills, was haranguing vehemently about rights of citizens, election, members of Congress, liberty, Bunker's Hill, heroes of seventy-six, and other words that were a perfect Babylonish jargon to the bewildered Van Winkle.

The appearance of Rip, with his long, grizzled beard, his rusty fowling-piece, his uncouth dress, and the army of women and children that had gathered at his heels, soon attracted the attention of the tavern politicians. They crowded round him, eying him from head to foot with great curiosity. The orator bustled up to him, and, drawing him partly aside, inquired on which side he voted. Rip stared in vacant stupidity. Another short but bushy little fellow pulled him by the arm, and, rising on tiptoe, inquired in his ear, whether he was Federal or Democrat. Rip was equally at a loss to comprehend the question ; when a knowing, self-important old gentleman, in a sharp cocked hat, made his way through the crowd, putting them to the right and left with his elbows as he passed, and planting himself before Van Winkle, with one arm a-kimbo, the other resting on his cane, his keen eyes and sharp hat penetrating as it were into his very soul, demanded in an austere tone what brought him to the election with a gun on his shoulder and a mob at his heels, and whether he meant to breed a riot in the village.

"Alas, gentlemen !" cried Rip, somewhat dismayed, "I am a poor, quiet man, a native of the place, and a loyal subject of the King, God bless him !"

Here a general shout burst from the bystanders : "A Tory ! a Tory ! a spy ! a refugee ! hustle him ! away with him !" It was with great difficulty that the self-important man in the cocked hat restored order ; and having assumed a tenfold austerity of brow, demanded again of the unknown culprit what he came there for, and whom he was seeking. The poor man humbly assured him that he meant no harm, but merely came there in search of some of his neighbors, who used to keep about the tavern.

"Well, who are they?—name them."

Rip bethought himself a moment, and inquired: "Where 's Nicholas Vedder?"

There was a silence for a little while, when an old man replied, in a thin, piping voice: "Nicholas Vedder? why, he is dead and gone these eighteen years. There was a wooden tombstone in the church-yard that used to tell all about him, but that 's rotten and gone too."

"Where 's Brom Dutcher?"

"Oh, he went off to the army in the beginning of the war; some say he was killed at the storming of Stony Point; others say he was drowned in the squall, at the foot of Antony's Nose. I don't know,—he never came back again."

"Where 's Van Bummel, the school-master?"

"He went off to the wars too, was a great militia-general, and is now in Congress."

Rip's heart died away at hearing of these sad changes in his home and friends, and finding himself thus alone in the world. Every answer puzzled him, too, by treating of such enormous lapses of time, and of matters which he could not understand,—war, Congress, Stony Point. He had no courage to ask after any more friends, but cried out in despair: "Does nobody here know Rip Van Winkle?"

"Oh! Rip Van Winkle!" exclaimed two or three; "Oh, to be sure! that 's Rip Van Winkle yonder, leaning against the tree!"

Rip looked, and beheld a precise counterpart of himself as he went up the mountain; apparently as lazy and certainly as ragged. The poor fellow was now completely confounded. He doubted his own identity, and whether he was himself or another man. In the midst of his bewilderment, the man in the cocked hat demanded who he was, and what was his name?

"God knows," exclaimed he, at his wit's end. "I 'm not myself, I 'm somebody else; that 's me yonder; no, that 's somebody else got into my shoes. I was myself last night; but I fell asleep on the mountain, and they 've changed my gun, and everything 's changed, and I 'm changed, and I can 't tell what 's my name, or who I am."

The bystanders began now to look at each other, nod, wink significantly, and tap their fingers against their foreheads. There was a whisper, also, about securing the gun, and keeping the old fellow from doing mischief; at the very suggestion of which the self-important man with the cocked hat retired with some precipitation. At this critical moment a fresh, comely woman passed through the throng to get a peep at the gray-bearded man. She had a chubby child in her arms, which, frightened at his looks, began to cry. "Hush, Rip," cried she, "hush, you little fool; the old man won't hurt you." The name of the child, the air of the mother, the tone of her voice, all awakened a train of recollections in his mind. "What is your name, my good woman?" asked he.

"Judith Gardenier."

"And your father's name?"

"Ah, poor man! his name was Rip Van Winkle; it 's twenty years since he went away from home with his gun, and never has been heard of since; his dog came home without him; but whether he shot himself, or was carried away by the Indians, nobody can tell. I was then but a little girl."

Rip had but one question more to ask; but he put it with a faltering voice:

" Where 's your mother ? "

" Oh, she too had died but a short time since : she broke a blood-vessel in a fit of passion at a New England pedlar."

There was a drop of comfort, at least, in this intelligence. The honest man could contain himself no longer. He caught his daughter and her child in his arms. " I am your father," cried he, —" Young Rip Van Winkle once,—old Rip Van Winkle now. Does nobody know poor Rip Van Winkle ? "

All stood amazed, until an old woman, tottering out from among the crowd, put her hand to her brow, and peering under it in his face for a moment, exclaimed : " Sure enough, it is Rip Van Winkle !—it is himself. Welcome home again, old neighbor. Why, where have you been these twenty long years ? "

Rip's story was soon told, for the whole twenty years had been to him but as one night. The neighbors stared when they heard it ; some were seen to wink at each other, and put their tongues in their cheeks ; and the self-important man in the cocked hat, who, when the alarm was over, had returned to the field, screwed down the corners of his mouth and shook his head,—upon which there was a general shaking of the head throughout the assemblage.

It was determined, however, to take the opinion of old Peter Vanderdonk, who was seen slowly advancing up the road. He was a descendant of the historian of that name, who wrote one of the earliest accounts of the province. Peter was the most ancient inhabitant of the village, and well versed in all the wonderful events and traditions of the neighborhood. He recollected Rip at once, and corroborated his story in the most satisfactory manner. He assured the company that it was a fact, handed down from his ancestor the historian, that the Kaatskill Mountains had always been haunted by strange beings ; that it was affirmed that the

great Hendrick Hudson, the first discoverer of the river and country, kept a kind of vigil there every twenty years, with his crew of
the Half Moon, being permitted in this way to revisit the scenes of
his enterprise, and keep a guardian eye upon the river and the
great city called by his name ; that his father had once seen them
in their old Dutch dresses playing at ninepins in a hollow of the
mountain ; and that he himself had heard, one summer afternoon,
the sound of their balls like distant peals of thunder.

To make a long story short, the company broke up, and returned to the more important concerns of the election. Rip's
daughter took him home to live with her ; she had a snug, well-
furnished house, and a stout, cheery farmer for a husband, whom
Rip recollected for one of the urchins that used to climb upon his
back. As to Rip's son and heir, who was the ditto of himself, seen
leaning against the tree, he was employed to work on the farm ;
but evinced a hereditary disposition to attend to any thing else
but his business.

Rip now resumed his old walks and habits ; he soon found
many of his former cronies, though all rather the worse for the
wear and tear of time ; and preferred making friends among the
rising generation, with whom he soon grew into great favor.

Having nothing to do at home, and being arrived at that happy
age when a man can do nothing with impunity, he took his place
once more on the bench, at the inn door, and was reverenced as
one of the patriarchs of the village, and a chronicle of the old
times "before the war." It was some time before he could get into the regular track of gossip, or could be made to comprehend
the strange events that had taken place during his torpor,—how
that there had been a revolutionary war ; that the country had
thrown off the yoke of old England ; and that, instead of being a
subject of His Majesty George III., he was now a free citizen of

the United States. Rip, in fact, was no politician ; the changes of states and empires made but little impression on him ; but there was one species of despotism under which he had long groaned, and that was petticoat government. Happily that was at an end ; he had got his neck out of the yoke of matrimony, and could go in and out whenever he pleased, without dreading the tyranny of Dame Van Winkle. Whenever her name was mentioned, however, he shook his head, shrugged his shoulders, and cast up his eyes ; which might pass either for an expression of resignation to his fate, or joy at his deliverance.

He used to tell his story to every stranger that arrived at Mr. Doolittle's hotel. He was observed, at first, to vary on some points every time he told it, which was doubtless owing to his having so recently awaked. It at last settled down precisely to the tale I have related ; and not a man, woman, or child in the neighborhood, but knew it by heart. Some always pretended to doubt the reality of it, and insisted that Rip had been out of his head, and that this was one point on which he always remained flighty. The old Dutch inhabitants, however, almost universally gave it full credit. Even to this day, they never hear a thunder-storm of a summer afternoon about the Kaatskill, but they say Hendrick Hudson and his crew are at their game of ninepins ; and it is a common wish of all henpecked husbands in the neighborhood, when life hangs heavy on their hands, that they might have a quieting **draught** out of Rip Van Winkle's flagon.

www.ingramcontent.com/pod-product-compliance
Lightning Source LLC
Chambersburg PA
CBHW021109020726
47500CB00003B/673